The secrets of Ms. Snickle's Class

The secrets of Ms. Snickle's Class

by Laurie Miller Hornik

illustrated by Debbie Tilley

Clarion Books
New York

Clarion Books
a Houghton Mifflin Company imprint
215 Park Avenue South, New York, NY 10003

The illustrations were executed in gouache and pen and ink.
The type was set in 14-point Berkeley Book.

www.houghtonmifflinbooks.com

Printed in USA

Library of Congress Cataloging-in-Publication Data

Hornik, Laurie Miller.
The secrets of Ms. Snickle's class / by Laurie Miller Hornik ;
illustrated by Debbie Tilley.
p. cm.
Summary: Every school has its secrets, but in Ms. Snickle's
classroom the secrets are extraordinary, and when Lacey sets out to
learn and tell them all, she puts Ms. Snickle's job in jeopardy.
ISBN 0-618-03435-8
[1. Secrets—Fiction. 2. Schools—Fiction. 3. Magic—Fiction.
4. Humorous stories.] I. Tilley, Debbie, ill. II. Title.

PZ7.H786 Se 2001
[Fic]—dc21 00-058979

QUM 10 9 8 7 6 5 4 3 2 1

For Rob and Ezra,
Mom and Dad,
and my third-grade students, 1992–98
—L. M. H.

For Gillian
—D. T.

Contents

chapter one

Eva's Secret

Eva had a long, elegant white neck, a proud black beak, and two strong wings. She was as magnificent as a swan, which is exactly what she was. Eva lived on a silver lake in a magical forest, which was also home to seven golden-hoofed deer, a tiny jeweled turtle that occasionally granted big wishes, and an evil sorcerer named Forgettit, who never did.

It was a lovely place to live. Unfortunately for Eva, she does not live there anymore, because Forgettit sent her away.

He had been trying to change her into a spider with his magic wand, but it's hard keeping all those spells straight. So Eva became a little girl instead. And when she saw what had happened to her, she did just what you or I would have done: She plopped down on the grass and cried. Her big silver tears made puddles filled with orange goldfish that leaped out of the water, desperately trying to cheer her up. At least five of the golden-hoofed deer rushed right over to see if they could help. But poor Eva just cried and cried. No one could do anything for her, and all her sniffling was beginning to get on the sorcerer's nerves.

So once again the evil sorcerer Forgettit pointed his magic wand at Eva. This time he took greater care with his spell, and with a loud *poof,* Eva the girl disappeared from the silver lake in the magical forest and suddenly found herself in Ms. Snickle's class in the Murmer Street School.

It is a terrible thing to be changed from a swan into a little girl and then *poof*ed to school. But Eva was lucky for two reasons.

First, she was lucky about the timing, because when she *poof*ed into the classroom, it was one minute before the start of school on the very first day of the new school year. It would have been much harder if she had appeared in the middle of the school year—or on a Saturday!

Second, she was lucky because the class she *poof*ed into was Ms. Snickle's class, and if ever there was a class where a little girl who

used to be a swan could feel comfortable, this was it.

The moment Eva appeared was that scary moment right before the day begins. All the children were whispering and wondering about what school would be like this year. Ms. Snickle was sitting at her desk at the front of the room, counting the students in her new class. All of a sudden—*poof!*—another little girl appeared in the room. She had pale silver hair and eyes like blue water, and she reminded Ms. Snickle of forests and castles and happy endings.

Hmm, Ms. Snickle thought. *How odd for a student to appear with a poof instead of walking through the door. Oh, well, it* is *the first day of school, and strange things do seem to happen on the first day of school.* She shrugged and began counting the students all over again.

Two children also happened to be watching the moment Eva *poof*ed in. Hayley saw Eva appear out of nowhere and instantly decided she liked this new girl. That was how Hayley was. She could always tell right away. Just as she was about to go over and say hello, she began a sneezing fit she couldn't stop. *Oh, dear,* thought Hayley, *and on the first day of school.*

Lacey also saw Eva appear out of nowhere and was instantly suspicious. How strange to just appear that way. Why couldn't she use the door like everybody else? Did she think she was special? And she had such odd hair, too.

Because of the magic, Eva did not remember that she had once been a swan. She carried a secret in her heart, one so heavy that magic must have been involved, and she felt strangely out of place in the classroom. Her stomach fluttered as she looked around at all the new faces. Then her eyes settled on Ms. Snickle and she felt oddly calm, like a feather being carried along on a summer breeze.

chapter two

Keeping Secrets

"Good morning, class," said Ms. Snickle. She walked around the room, smiling at her new students. A faint scent seemed to follow her as she walked.

She smells like wet cat fur, thought Nathan.

She smells like ice cream, thought Oliver.

She smells like magic, thought Eva.

She smells! thought Lacey.

ACHOO! sneezed Hayley, and she thought, *Whatever that smell is, it's making me sneeze!*

Ms. Snickle went to her desk and stood next to a big pile of booklets.

"Here we go again," Dennis mumbled.

Hayley leaned over to Eva. "You're new, so you don'd know, bud every year we have doo dake a desd on the firsd day of sgool doo zee wud we forgod ober the subber. ACHOO!"

"Bird bless you," said Eva, but Hayley's ears were stuffed up, so it sounded like "God bless you."

Eva tried to remember what she had forgotten over the summer, but she couldn't remember.

Oliver whispered to Nathan, "That test is stupid. It's stupid that we have to take it."

Lacey overheard. Lacey loved to tattle. In fact, last year kids had started calling her Lacey the tattletale, but then Lacey told on them and they had to stop. This opportunity was too good to waste. She raised her hand.

"Ms. Snickle, Oliver said the test is *stupid* and that it's *stupid* that we have to take it."

"Oh, did he now?" said Ms. Snickle. Oliver slumped down in his seat.

"Oliver, what do you have to say for yourself?"

"Well, I mean . . . I didn't mean . . . It's just, everyone thinks tests are stup—I mean . . ." He tried to think of a word for stupid that would be okay to say to a teacher, but he couldn't think of any. "I mean, they're just not fun."

"Not fun." Ms. Snickle repeated his words. Some of the kids nodded a teeny bit, because it was true, but mostly they didn't, because they didn't want to get in trouble.

"Oliver," said Ms. Snickle, "please come to my desk."

Oliver wriggled out of his seat and walked as slowly as possible to the front of the room. He didn't know what was going to happen, but he figured it would be pretty bad. In his experience, teachers did not call you to their desk for good things.

"I have a job for you," Ms. Snickle said. She picked up the test booklets and put them into Oliver's arms. They were very heavy. Oliver staggered a bit but stood his ground.

"Do you know what to do with them?" she asked.

"Pass them out?" Oliver asked meekly.

"Of course not!" Ms. Snickle laughed. "Throw those stupid tests into the recycling box. I never liked them, either. I thought you kids liked them!"

A chorus of relieved *No*s rose in the room.

"It's so strange," said Ms. Snickle. "If kids don't like tests, and teachers don't like tests, I wonder why schools have so many of them?"

No one knew.

"Oh, well." Ms. Snickle glanced at the clock. "The test was going to take an hour, so I guess we'd better have free time instead. Would that be okay?"

Everyone nodded. Free time was their best subject.

Everyone immediately began not working. They took free time very seriously. Dennis and Nathan were hanging out at the electric pencil sharpener. They were having a contest to see who could make a sharper pencil point.

"You won that round," said Nathan. It was true. Dennis's pencil point really *was* sharper. They jammed their pencils down on the table, breaking the points, to get ready for the next round. You had to start with no point or it wasn't fair.

Eva felt very alone. She looked around for someone to talk to, but Hayley had gone to the nurse, and Eva felt too shy to approach any of the other children. She ended up sitting in a corner with some origami paper. She began absent-mindedly folding it this way and that, and before she knew it, she had made a turtle, a fish, and a deer. They felt strangely familiar.

Oliver was sitting at his desk, trying to make

the perfect paper airplane. So far he hadn't had much luck. But it wasn't his fault. His teacher last year had not spent enough time teaching the fine art of making paper airplanes.

Lacey looked around the room. "Looking for trouble," some people called it, but Lacey didn't see it that way. She didn't go looking for trouble. She and trouble just seemed to enjoy the same things. For instance, right now there was a big crowd around the pencil sharpener. That meant trouble. So Lacey picked up her pencil, broke off the point, and went to stand in the pencil-sharpener line.

It wasn't really a line, Lacey realized. It was more of a circle. Nathan was in the middle and everyone else was gathered around watching. The sharp-pencil-point contest was over, and a new activity had started. Nathan had dumped all the pencil shavings from the sharpener onto the floor and was carefully swirling them with the end of a paper clip to make designs. He had made a cat, some broccoli, and something that looked like a swan. Or maybe a girl. It was hard to tell.

Everyone was so busy admiring the designs that no one noticed Ms. Snickle come up and join the circle.

"Nathan!" Ms. Snickle said. "Are you responsible for this?"

They all froze. Nathan gulped. "I'll clean it up," he offered hopefully.

"Clean it up?" said Ms. Snickle. "Nonsense! This is beautiful! I just love the broccoli one! Broccoli is my favorite vegetable."

The kids were too stunned even to say "Ew."

Ms. Snickle called the rest of the class over to admire Nathan's designs. Everyone oohed and aahed. Lacey couldn't believe her ears. It was strange enough that Ms. Snickle didn't like tests, but who ever heard of a teacher who liked messes!

Just then Hayley returned from the nurse. She carried some extra tissues, since she was still sneezing.

Lacey had an idea.

"Hayley! Come look at what Nathan made."

Hayley hurried over. "Wud?" she asked between sneezes.

Ms. Snickle also had an idea. "Uh, just wait right there, Hayley. It's not quite done." Ms. Snickle ran to her supply closet and came back with a spray can.

"Stand back!" she warned the kids. They stood back. Ms. Snickle pointed the nozzle of the can at Nathan's designs and sprayed them thoroughly.

"Okay, Hayley, you can look now."

"Wow! Wud cool dezignz!" Hayley said. "Uh-oh, I think I'b going doo . . . ah . . . ah . . . ah . . ."

"DON'T SNEEZE!" wailed Nathan. "YOU'LL WRECK IT!"

Hayley couldn't help it. ACHOO! she sneezed.

All the kids shut their eyes. They couldn't bear to look. They imagined pencil shavings flying all over the room.

"It's okay, children. You can look," said Ms. Snickle.

Slowly the children began to open their eyes and utter relieved sighs. The designs were still there. The swan (if it was a swan) had shut its eyes, and the broccoli was a tiny bit soggy, but other than that they looked perfect.

"But how did you . . . ?" Lacey couldn't finish her sentence.

Ms. Snickle held up her spray can. The label read:

PENCIL SHAVING FIXATIVE—APPLY GENEROUSLY
TO PERMANENTLY SAVE PENCIL-SHAVING DESIGNS
WATERPROOF, ERASER-PROOF, AND DEFINITELY SNEEZE-PROOF

Free time was over. Ms. Snickle hung the designs next to the chalkboard while the children sat back down at their desks.

"Class," Ms. Snickle said, using a serious voice the children had not yet heard. "You may have noticed that there don't seem to be very many rules in this classroom."

They had noticed. The children smiled and nodded.

"Before we go on, I need to tell you the one

important rule I do have." A few kids groaned. After all, rules were never any fun.

Ms. Snickle went to the chalkboard, chose a purple piece of chalk, and wrote in clear, large letters NO TELLING SECRETS.

"ACHOO," sneezed Hayley.

"God bless you, Hayley," said Ms. Snickle.

Eva felt a little flutter deep in her belly. *I wonder what that is?* she thought.

Nathan raised his hand. "We had that rule in my class last year," he said. "No Secrets. I remember it came right after No Spitting."

"Oh, my! You had a No Secrets rule! That's awful!" said Ms. Snickle.

The children were confused. Didn't Ms. Snickle just say she had the same rule?

"You see," Ms. Snickle explained, "our class rule isn't No Secrets. It's No *Telling* Secrets. They are very different rules. They are as different as . . . as . . . chocolate ice cream with strawberry sauce and strawberry ice cream with chocolate sauce, as different as pink lizards with purple spots and purple lizards with pink spots."

The children nodded. Ms. Snickle had a wonderful way of explaining things.

"Secrets are very important," Ms. Snickle went on. "Everyone has them." A few kids giggled and blushed. Others tried to look very serious, as if they didn't know what she was talking about. Eva *really* didn't know what her teacher was talking about, but she felt that little flutter in her stomach again. *That must be what a secret feels like,* she thought. It felt as if it were trying to get out.

"Now, are there any questions?" Ms. Snickle asked.

There were lots of questions. Why do you care so much about secrets? What will happen if we tell them? How do you know everybody has secrets? Do you know what our secrets are? Yes, there were lots of questions, but no one asked them. It felt funny to be talking about secrets, especially with a teacher.

At the end of the day, Ms. Snickle wrote the homework on the board. WRITING ASSIGNMENT: SECRETS ARE VERY IMPORTANT. THINK ABOUT YOUR OWN SECRETS AS WELL AS SECRETS IN GENERAL.

What strange homework, thought the children. But they had noticed that there were a lot of strange things about Ms. Snickle's class. Mostly, they were just happy that they didn't have to do any math problems. They took out their pencils and copied the assignment carefully into their notebooks.

Lacey took out her pencil, but it still didn't have a point. She hadn't gotten to sharpen it, and she didn't feel like getting up again. She felt around in the back of her desk and found a little hand-held pencil sharpener she had brought from home. It wasn't as good as the electric one, but she used it anyway and dumped the shavings in her desk. She did *not* make designs out of them.

chapter three

Ms. Snickle's Secret

At 3:10 p.m. all the children packed their book bags and left the classroom. They took their secrets with them. Some of the children went straight home. Some went to their cello lessons. Eva walked across the street to the park.

She had never been there before but felt somehow that it was where she belonged. She skipped to the edge of a little pond. Dozens of happy, quacky ducks were skimming the water and sharing duck thoughts. Near them some pigeons were cooing away about the day. Eva settled comfortably against a tree near the pond. She rested her head on her book bag and took a nap filled with flying-swan dreams.

At 3:27, Ms. Snickle picked up her purse and left the classroom. She walked down the two flights of stairs, waved good-bye to Jimmy at the front desk and walked down the front steps of the school.

Ms. Snickle did not go home. She did not go to a cello lesson or to the park. Instead, she walked to the supermarket. She bought two pints of lollipop–lima bean ice cream and some broccoli. Ms. Snickle thought eating healthy was very important.

By the time Ms. Snickle returned, all the children had left the school. She came in through the basement entrance, tiptoed up to her classroom on the third floor, and opened the door. She carefully unpacked her groceries. She put the ice cream into Nathan's desk. Then she pressed her secret button and blinked.

In exactly one blink of an eye the room changed, just as it did every afternoon. Nathan's desk became Ms. Snickle's freezer, and Lacey's desk turned into her bed. Oliver's desk turned into her couch, and Dennis's desk turned into a TV set. The other desks turned into a coffee table, a closet, a bathtub, an alarm clock, a sink, a telephone, and a black and gray cat named Shirley.

This was where Ms. Snickle lived. That was her secret. She did not have an apartment in the city or

a house in the suburbs. When she pressed the secret button, her classroom became her apartment.

And it wasn't just the desks that changed. The fluorescent lights turned into sparkling chandeliers that dropped elegantly from the ceiling. The bulletin boards on the walls shimmered and became beautiful oil paintings in fancy gold frames. The floorboards shivered, and a red and purple Oriental rug with a beautiful flower-and-vine pattern appeared.

Ms. Snickle looked around. "That's better!" she exclaimed. She lay down on Oliver's desk (which was really her couch) and turned on Dennis's desk (which was really her TV). She petted Hayley's desk (which was really her cat, Shirley, and which had come over to rub against her leg). She looked at Lacey's desk (which was really her bed) and at the orange-flowered pillows covered with pencil shavings. She sighed.

"I hope Lacey won't keep leaving so many pencil shavings in her desk!" she exclaimed. "They do get stuck in my hair."

chapter four

Oliver's Secret

OLIVER

I have a secret. You probably already know that, because you seem to know a lot about secrets. Last night I was so nervous about school that I wet my bed. Since our class rule is No Telling Secrets, I know you won't tell anyone my secret. I can see that you really understand about secrets.

DENNIS

Secrets are very tricky things. **If** you tell a secret, is it still a secret? **Is** a secret something that nobody else knows, or that most people don't know? What if you tell a secret, but nobody believes you? Then have you told a secret or not? **If** a tree falls in a forest and nobody hears it, does it make a noise? **I** don't know what that has to do with secrets, but it is an interesting question!

EVA

There is a little flutter in my stomach. I think it might be my secret trying to get out.

HAYLEY

Please excuse this mess. I ran out of tissues, so I had to use my homework.

LACEY

Secrets are very important. The most important thing about secrets is discovering them. There are many ways to do this:

1. Spy on people on their way to school.
2. Spy on people on their way home from school.
3. Spy on people during school.
4. Use technology.
5. If you're lucky, a secret might even fall into your lap.

P.S. You might be right that everyone else has secrets, but not me.

NATHAN

Our class rule is No Telling Secrets. I have a secret, but I'm not telling.

As the children came in the next morning, they took their homework to Ms. Snickle's desk, looking for a basket to put it in. They had learned to do that in school last year. Eva had never been to school before, of course, but she watched the other kids and did what they did.

Ms. Snickle laughed. "Oh, no, class, please don't give your papers to me. They're not mine! They're yours to keep at home. That's why it's called *home*-work. If you were supposed to bring it to school, it would be called *school*work." Ms. Snickle smiled sweetly and shook her head. There were so many things the children didn't know.

"I hope you enjoyed writing about secrets," she continued. "Since they're yours, you can do what you wish with them. Just remember: Secrets are precious and sometimes a bit fragile, so be careful!"

Uncertainly, the children began to stuff their papers into their pockets or in the back of their notebooks, hiding them. From then on their home-work never took as long to do, and they never made the mistake of trying to hand it in again.

chapter five

Nathan's Secret

"My zizder is *zo* grozz. She eads with her toes," Hayley whispered.

"Ew!" said the children.

"Oh, that's *nothing!*" said Oliver. "My little brother lets the *dog* lick his *nose.*"

"Ew!" said the children.

"I can beat all of you," said Lacey. "My little brother once mixed together two eggs, shells and all, raisins, and shampoo—and *ate it!* We had to call poison control. For a week he burped bubbles that smelled like raw eggs and raisins."

"Ew!" said the children.

By now all the children in Ms. Snickle's class were gathered around, ew-ing loudly. None of the other children had little brothers and sisters, except for Nathan. He had a little sister, but he hoped no one would ask him about her. It was a secret.

"I sdill thingk eading with your toes is grozzezd," said Hayley.

"No way!" said Lacey.

"Yes way!"

"Unh-unh!"

"Uh-huh!"

"Let's ask Ms. Snickle!" the children cried.

"Ms. Sdiggle!" Hayley called out. "Whij is grozzer: ledding a dog lig your doze or eading with your toes?"

"No, *that's* not the question," said Lacey. "The question is, Which is grosser: Eating with your toes or burping bubbles that smell like raw eggs and raisins?"

Ms. Snickle brushed some pencil shavings out of her hair. "My goodness!" she said. "Are people in our class doing these things? Maybe we need a few more rules, after all."

"No, no one in our class does such gross things. It's our brothers and sisters. We're trying to figure out who has the grossest brother or sister."

"Oh, I see. Well, in that case . . . hmm . . . it is a very difficult question. However, I think it is quite obvious what we should do now."

"Stop talking and do our work?" asked Dennis.

"What? No! Of course not. What a silly idea! This is much too important. We will need to have a Gross Brother and Sister Contest. Everyone who has a brother or sister will bring them in tomorrow for sharing time and have them do their grossest thing."

Instead of teaching the class about fractions, Ms. Snickle let the students get ready for the Gross Brother and Sister Contest in little groups. Those who didn't have brothers or sisters helped the other kids plan.

"Can I work with you?" Eva asked Oliver. Eva didn't have any brothers or sisters. At least she didn't think she did. She couldn't remember exactly.

"Sure!" said Oliver. "Let's see . . . I'll need to bring my little brother, Licky, and my dog, Lucky."

"I can meet you and help you bring them to school if you want," Eva offered.

"Don't you have to get permission to meet me before school?" asked Oliver.

Eva shrugged. "I don't think it will be a problem." She thought about asking permission from the ducks and pigeons she slept near in the park, but she really didn't think they would mind.

Dennis didn't have any brothers or sisters either, so he helped Hayley get ready for the contest. Her little sister Tozy's favorite food was peas. She would put them between her toes and suck them out one by one. Dennis offered to bring the peas. Hayley would bring her sister.

Lacey planned for her brother Bubba's performance all by herself. She would bring eggs, raisins, and shampoo. Some kids offered to help, but Lacey said no. She wanted to win all by herself.

"Oh, Nathan!" said Ms. Snickle. "Don't you have a little sister, too? I am certainly looking forward to meeting her. I'm sure she'll do really gross things. What are you thinking of having her do?"

"Uh . . . uh . . . uh . . . I have to go to the bathroom," Nathan said, and ran out of the classroom.

Nathan sat in one of the bathroom stalls. He didn't know what to do. He didn't think his little sister was gross. In fact, he kind of liked her. It was a secret. He didn't want to let anyone find out. It was so embarrassing. Who ever heard of liking your sister!

Maybe he'd have to tell. What choice did he have? But then Nathan remembered something. He

reached into his pocket and pulled out a piece of paper. It was the homework assignment from the first day of school. He read it over. OUR CLASS RULE IS NO TELLING SECRETS. I HAVE A SECRET, BUT I'M NOT TELLING. He couldn't tell his secret even if he wanted to, because he would be breaking the rule. Maybe he would just not bring his sister. It was his only choice, really. *Yeah, that should do it,* he thought. He walked back to class.

At the end of the day Ms. Snickle read off the names of the children who had little brothers and sisters. "Oliver, Hayley, Lacey, and Nathan. Now, I expect to see all of them here in school tomorrow. Don't forget! We have to be able to see each brother or sister so we can vote fairly on which one is grossest. I am particularly curious to see what Nathan's little sister does, since he hasn't told us about it yet."

"YEAH!" everyone shouted.

Nathan gulped. *I guess I'll have to bring her, after all,* he thought.

The next morning all the kids in Ms. Snickle's class were very excited. Some of them had had a hard time sneaking their little sisters and brothers out of the house.

Lacey tried the direct approach. She had said, "Mom and Dad, tomorrow we are having a Gross Brother and Sister Contest at school, so is it okay if I bring Bubba?"

"Certainly," her father had said.

"Sure," said her mother. "Hey, hon, why don't you have him do the trick where he burps raisins and raw eggs. That'll win for sure."

"Yeah," her father agreed, "that really is gross."

Eva met Oliver in the lobby of his building, as she had promised.

WOOF! WOOF! WOOF! WOOF! Oliver's dog Lucky went crazy as soon as he saw Eva.

"Down, Lucky!" Oliver cried. "I'm sorry, Eva. I don't understand it. Lucky never barks at people. Sometimes at pigeons, but never at people."

Eva sighed. Her secret fluttered around a bit, but as Lucky finally calmed down, her secret did, too.

Oliver's brother, Licky, greeted Eva in the usual way, by licking her nose.

"Ewww!" said Eva.

Oliver grinned. "Save it for the contest."

Ms. Snickle blinked the lights for quiet. She brushed some pencil shavings out of her hair.

"Lacey," she said, "you really must keep your desk cleaner." Then she continued. "Everyone, the Gross Brother and Sister Contest is about to begin. Take careful note as each student shows off the grossest thing his or her brother or sister does. I'll use my special ew-meter to measure how loudly you all shout 'Ew.' Whoever gets the loudest 'Ew' wins, and that brother or sister will be declared the grossest one."

Oliver went first with Licky. He took Lucky out of a box. Lucky bounded toward Licky. Licky giggled.

Then Lucky licked Licky on the nose. Licky laughed loudly. Lucky drooled on Licky. Licky drooled on Lucky. It was very wet and yucky.

"Ew!" cried the children. Ms. Snickle studied her ew-meter. Ten was the loudest. Licky scored an eight.

Next up was Hayley. Hayley sat her sister, Tozy, on top of Ms. Snickle's desk. In front of her she placed a plate of peas.

"Go, Dozy!" shouted Hayley.

Tozy put a pea between her big toe and her second toe. Then she placed one between her second toe and middle toe. She put a third one between her middle and fourth toes, and then a little pea between her fourth and baby toes.

All the children were grossed out already. None of them could take their eyes off her.

Tozy raised her pudgy foot. She put it against her mouth, then SLURP SLURP SLURP SLURP, the peas were gone.

"EW!!!" the children shouted. Ms. Snickle held the ew-meter up to the light so she could read it exactly.

"Nine and a half," she announced.

Next up was Lacey's little brother, Bubba. Lacey had everyone sit close so they would be able to smell Bubba's burp. They watched as Bubba broke the eggs into a bowl and mixed them all up, including the shells. Then Bubba added the shampoo and the raisins. He raised the bowl up and gulped the mixture down.

"Ew!" some kids called out.

"Six!" read Ms. Snickle.

"He's not done!" Lacey shouted. "Just wait."

Everyone waited. In a moment they saw a little shudder go through Bubba's body. It was a burp in the making. All of a sudden Bubba opened his mouth and let out a tremendous burp. It was caught inside a huge soap bubble. It drifted toward Oliver and then back over toward Eva. It caught a little breeze and twirled around toward Hayley and then back around toward Dennis. It was hanging over the middle of the circle of children when all of a sudden . . . POP!

The smell was disgusting! Raw eggs and raisins and soap and traces of Bubba's dinner from last night—broccoli and lamb chops.

The class went crazy. *"EW!!!!!"* the children all shouted as they held their noses.

"Bubba scored a perfect ten!" Ms. Snickle announced.

"Well, then it's over," said Lacey. "I win!"

"It's not over yet," said Ms. Snickle. "We still need to see Nathan's sister. She could tie with Bubba."

"That's all right," said Nathan. "I don't mind not having a turn. We can just call Lacey the winner."

"Nonsense," said Ms. Snickle. "Your sister needs to have a turn. Otherwise, we will never know for absolute sure whose brother or sister is grossest. We have to finish the contest."

Nathan took his little sister, Suzy, up to the front of the room and stood her on Ms. Snickle's desk. He stood next to her on the floor. He had no idea what to do. Suzy didn't really do anything very gross or awful. She was really cute. Nathan stared out at the class and waited for an idea to come to him. All of a sudden Suzy threw her arms around Nathan and gave him a huge kiss on the cheek.

"EEEEEEEWWWWWW!" all the kids shouted. Lacey fainted. Dennis and Oliver ran for the door. Hayley hid under her desk. Eva wondered if Nathan would turn into a frog.

Ms. Snickle held up the ew-meter. She watched the little light. Up it went, past the six, the seven, the eight, the nine. It hit the ten. Then it burst right out of the machine. The ew-meter exploded and went dead.

Nathan was declared the winner, and everyone except Lacey congratulated him.

"No hard feelings," Oliver said. "I just feel sorry for you having such a gross sister. I wouldn't trade with you for anything."

chapter six

Secrets Are Like Bubblegum

Lacey was chewing gum. She loved chewing gum. She loved the feeling of the squishy sugary glob against her teeth. She loved stretching the gum into long strings and swirling the strings around her tongue. She especially loved blowing bubbles. But Lacey couldn't blow bubbles in school because she couldn't even chew gum. There was a rule: No Chewing Gum. It wasn't a *class* rule. It was a *school* rule.

In the whole Murmer Street School, no one was allowed to chew gum. Mrs. Hevelheed, the principal, had made the rule. She knew that it was very important not to let children chew gum. She had learned that in principal school. She didn't remember why it was so important, but that didn't matter. If she learned it in principal school, it had to be important.

Lacey liked blowing bubbles because it was just like having a secret. The fun part about blowing a bubble was showing it off, just like with a secret. The bigger it was, the better. Of course, inside it was just a lot of hot air, and in the end it usually popped back in your face. But still, Lacey loved secrets . . . and bubblegum.

In the principal's office Mrs. Hevelheed's nose began to twitch.

"Gum!" she cried out. "I smell gum!" Her face got pink, although not as pink as Lacey's gum. A small amount of smoke escaped out her ears.

"Somewhere in my school someone is chewing gum! Someday I will find that person, and when I do . . . !" Mrs. Hevelheed cackled unpleasantly as she thought of all the things she would do when she found the chewer. She spun her swivel chair around to face her favorite poster. It hung right over her desk. On it was a picture of an angry tooth with the words NO GUM above it. Mrs. Hevelheed smiled as she looked at the poster. She had gotten it at the principal store. It had been hard to get because so many principals had wanted it, but she had wanted it the most.

"No gum, no gum, no gum," she sang. Getting to tell children that was one of her favorite parts of being a principal. She remembered the very first time she said it to a child.

"No gum!" she had barked. The child had been so nervous he had sort of choked on the gum and then swallowed it. "I said," Mrs. Hevelheed had yelled at the poor, unfortunate boy, "NO GUM!"

"But . . . but . . . I don't have any gum in my mouth, Mrs. Hevelheed," the quavering boy had said as politely as he could. He opened his mouth to show her.

"It's true that you don't have any gum in your mouth," Mrs. Hevelheed had agreed, "but you have gum in your stomach. And it takes seven years to fully digest a piece of gum, so I am afraid that I will have to suspend you from school for seven years."

Oh, what fun that had been!

Mrs. Hevelheed looked at the clock. It was 2:43 p.m. A perfect time to go on a gum-finding mission. She opened her desk drawer and pulled out a magnismelling glass—it was like a regular magnifying glass, but instead of making things look bigger, it made things *smell* bigger. It would help her smell out any gum chewers.

Mrs. Hevelheed held the magnismelling glass in front of her nose and followed the sugary scent down the hall and up the stairs.

Ms. Snickle could hear her coming. She was using her special magnihearing glass. It was like a magnismelling glass, but instead of making things smell bigger, it made them sound louder.

"Children," she said, "Mrs. Hevelheed is on her way. I think this would be a good time for anyone who is chewing gum to dispose of it properly." She handed out little pieces of paper for kids to wrap their gum in.

"No, thank you," said Dennis. Dennis did not need a piece of paper, because he wasn't chewing gum. Dennis never chewed gum. His mother didn't approve of gum chewing. She said it was bad for your teeth.

That's odd, thought Lacey. She'd never met anyone who didn't chew gum. Even Ms. Snickle was wrapping up her own gum in a piece of paper.

Why doesn't Dennis ever chew gum? Lacey wondered. She smelled a secret, almost as sweet as her bubblegum. But right now she had her own problem . . . what should she do with her gum?

Nathan said, "Oh, I don't need a piece of paper,

either, Ms. Snickle. I can just put it behind my ear."

"Oh, I really wouldn't," said Ms. Snickle. "It could get stuck in your hair, and then you would have to use peanut butter to get it out."

"EEEEWWW!" said all of the children. If Ms. Snickle's ew-meter had been working, it would have recorded at least a six, but unfortunately it was still at the ew-meter shop getting repaired.

Lacey didn't know what to do. She didn't want to put the gum behind her ear and have it get stuck in her hair. She looked at the little piece of paper Ms. Snickle had given her. She didn't want to waste the gum by wrapping it in paper. The gum would stick to the paper and then she couldn't chew it again. And it was her last piece!

Lacey had to think fast. She could hear Mrs. Hevelheed coming closer. Lacey pulled the gum out of her mouth and stuck it under her desk. She folded the piece of paper Ms. Snickle had given her into a fan and frantically began to fan the gum. Lacey knew a lot about gum. She knew that gum smells like gum only when you're chewing it. If you take it out of your mouth and let it dry up, it doesn't smell anymore. She hoped fanning the gum would make it dry very quickly.

Mrs. Hevelheed burst into the room. "GUM!" she yelled. She held out her magnismelling glass and sniffed long and hard. "I SMELL GUM!" she yelled, then stopped suddenly. "But the smell isn't coming from in here, after all." She whipped around and followed her nose down the hall. "Wherever you are," she called, "I'll find you, and when I do . . . !" Her voice got softer as she went farther down the hall. Ms. Snickle put away her magnihearing glass and breathed a sigh of relief.

"That was close," she said. A few children looked forlornly at the garbage pail, filled with their gum, all wrapped in paper and ruined.

"Oh, my!" said Ms. Snickle. "It's already time to go home."

Indeed it was. Bubblegumless, all the kids ran to their lockers to get their book bags and cellos. Everyone except Lacey.

Lacey stayed where she was, peeling the gum off the bottom of her desk. At least she *tried* to peel it, but it wouldn't peel. It was really, really stuck.

"Oh, well," Lacey sighed glumly. "I guess I'll have to buy a new piece, after all." She waved good-bye to Ms. Snickle, grabbed her book bag, and left.

* * *

At 3:27, Ms. Snickle picked up her purse and left the classroom, too, just as she always did. She walked down the two flights of stairs, waved good-bye to Jimmy, and continued out of the school.

She hurried to the supermarket. All that talk about gum had made her especially hungry. She bought three pints of bubblegum–brussels sprout ice cream. She rushed back to the school, stuck two of the ice cream containers in Nathan's desk (which was really her freezer), and pressed her secret button. Around her the stark classroom shimmered and became her comfortable apartment. Ms. Snickle sighed happily. She scooped some ice cream into Shirley's dish, then sat contentedly with the container in her lap and had her mid-afternoon snack.

A few minutes later Ms. Snickle yawned. "Shirley," she said. "Today was a long, hard day. I think, if you don't mind, I might take a nap." Shirley didn't mind. Ms. Snickle gave her the rest of the container of ice cream and plopped down on her bed (which was really Lacey's desk).

"EEEEWWWW!" said Ms. Snickle. If the ew-meter had been working, it would have recorded at least a seven.

"Shirley, something is stuck to my hair!" Shirley and Ms. Snickle examined her hair. It was gum. They looked at the pillow. Gum was stuck all over the orange flowers.

"Oh, Lacey," Ms. Snickle said. "I know you love your gum, but I do wish you wouldn't put it under your desk." Then to Shirley she said, "I guess I'll be

making one more trip to the supermarket, after all." Shirley licked up a chunk of brussels sprout from the ice cream and meowed.

Ms. Snickle and Shirley spent most of the night over a jar of peanut butter. Ms. Snickle spooned it onto her hair and rubbed it in, and then Shirley licked it off. It was slow work. It was four in the morning by the time they had gotten the last of the gum out of her hair. Ms. Snickle and Shirley slept curled up together on a pillow covered with yellow flowers. Ms. Snickle liked her orange-flowered pillowcase better, but she had had to send it out overnight to be cleaned. The next day it was back, as good as new, but Ms. Snickle's hair smelled like peanut butter for two weeks.

chapter seven

Hayley's Secret

Ms. Snickle's class was practicing their pizza toppings spellings, because, as Ms. Snickle always said, "Pizza is more fun when you know how to spell the toppings."

Eva went first. "Spell 'cheese,'" said Ms. Snickle.

"C-h-e-e-s-e."

"Very good," said Ms. Snickle, smiling. Eva had learned a lot in school already. The first day she hadn't been able to spell anything, but now she could spell lots of hard words. There was still something a bit odd about her, but Ms. Snickle didn't give it much thought. After all, everyone had secrets, and as long as they didn't hurt anybody, Ms. Snickle thought that was just fine.

"ACHOO!" sneezed Hayley loudly.

"God bless you, Hayley," said Ms. Snickle. "Oliver, are you ready for your turn?"

Oliver nodded.

"Spell 'pepperoni.'"

"Q-l-x-x-z," said Oliver. He had never been a very good speller.

"ACHOO!" sneezed Hayley loudly.

"God bless you, Hayley," said Ms. Snickle. "I'm sorry, Oliver. That's wrong. I'm not sure how to spell it, either, but I know there must be at least two or three *p*'s in it somewhere.

"Hayley, it's your turn. Here's an easy one. Spell 'tomato.'"

"D-o-m-a-d-ACHOO!-o," said Hayley.

"I'm sorry, Hayley. That's wrong. There are two *t*'s in tomato, not two *d*'s. And I am quite certain there is no 'ACHOO.'"

"Thad'z wud I zed," said Hayley. "By doze iz zduvd ub. Bay I go doo the durze?"

"I think that's a good idea," said Ms. Snickle.

Hayley walked to Nurse Wellhead's office. It was down two flights of stairs, through three doors, and around a corner. Hayley did not have to guide her feet, though. She went to the nurse so much that her feet automatically took her there. Sometimes when she was trying to go to the gym or the library she would find herself accidentally headed toward Nurse Wellhead's office instead. It was her second home.

Hayley walked in.

"Hi, Hayley. I thought I heard you sniffling in the hall," Nurse Wellhead said.

Hayley explained, "I keeb sneezig ad by doze iz zduvd ub."

"I can't understand what you are saying," Nurse Wellhead said. "Your nose is too stuffed up. Here, drink this." She gave Hayley a cup of pink liquid with green bubbles in it. Hayley drank it. It smelled like cotton candy and tasted like lemonade.

"If you don't feel better in an hour, come back."

When Hayley got back to her classroom, Ms. Snickle was teaching a science lesson about imaginary animals.

"Who knows how many teeth unicorns have?" asked Ms. Snickle.

"ACHOO!" sneezed Hayley loudly.

"Eighteen," answered Dennis. Dennis knew a lot about teeth.

"Okay," said Ms. Snickle. "One more hard one. What kind of noise does a sea monster make when it has a cold?"

"ACHOO!" sneezed Hayley.

"Very good, Hayley," said Ms. Snickle.

"I thig," said Hayley, "thad I'd bedder go bag doo the durze."

Hayley walked down the two flights of stairs. She felt dizzy from all her sneezing. In her mind sea monsters and unicorns and dragons danced around, sneezing and blowing their noses.

Hayley walked through the three doors and into Nurse Wellhead's office.

"I'b zdill sneezig," she announced.

"I see," said Nurse Wellhead. "Here, swallow these." She gave Hayley two pills. Hayley swallowed them. They smelled like chocolate and tasted like potato chips.

"Come back in an hour if you're not better."

Hayley headed upstairs. *What's wrong with me?* she wondered glumly. *I never sneeze at home. Only at school. And I never used to sneeze at school. Just this year. How can I have a cold only during the day and never at night or on weekends? It doesn't make any sense.*

Hayley walked into her classroom.

The class was having a math lesson. The children were estimating how many pencil shavings

Lacey had in her desk. Nathan was whispering something to Oliver as Hayley passed him on her way to her seat.

"ACHOO!" sneezed Hayley. And then, "ACHOO ACHOO ACHOO ACHOO ACHOO!" She was sneezing uncontrollably.

Pencil shavings flew everywhere, especially all over Lacey.

"Watch where you sneeze!" Lacey said angrily, brushing the soggy shavings off her shirt.

Ms. Snickle sent Hayley back down to Nurse Wellhead right away, even though it hadn't been an hour.

Nurse Wellhead sat Hayley down. "I think," said Nurse Wellhead, "you must be allergic to something. The question is . . . what?"

"How gan we fide oud?" asked Hayley.

"There's a special way to test for allergies," Nurse Wellhead explained. "What we do is rub a little bit of what we think you might be allergic to directly onto your skin, and if you get a little rash, it means you are allergic. For instance, if you are allergic to milk and we rub some onto your skin, you would get a little rash there and we'd know it's milk, so you would stop drinking it."

"Id'z nod milk," Hayley said. "I dringk milk ad hobe ad I dever sneeze ad hobe."

"You never sneeze ad hobe—I mean, at home?" asked Nurse Wellhead. "That's very interesting." She wrote it in a little blue notebook. "That's very good. That means we can rule out many things. We know, for instance, that you are not allergic to your little brother."

"I don'd have a liddle brother."

"Even better!" exclaimed Nurse Wellhead, writing it in her notebook. "Then it is even more certain. We also know that you are not allergic to your parents or your pets or your living room rug or your brand of bubble bath." As Nurse Wellhead said each item, she listed it in her notebook.

"You're also not allergic to watching TV or talking on the telephone or eating breakfast or brushing your teeth." Nurse Wellhead kept writing. She was on the seventeenth page of her list of things Hayley could not be allergic to when Hayley finally interrupted.

"Bud, Nurse Wellhead, wud *am* I allergig doo?"

"Let's see, it would have to be something in your classroom," said Nurse Wellhead, "because you

sneeze the most in there. Let me see your arms."
Hayley held out her arms.

"There's enough room on each arm to test five things," Nurse Wellhead explained. "So we can test ten things altogether. First I need to prepare your arms." She took Hayley's right arm and cleaned it carefully with a gauze pad soaked in alcohol. Then with a felt-tipped pen she drew five circles and numbered them one, two, three, four, and five.

"That's so we can remember later where we tested each thing, and can determine what you are allergic to." Next Nurse Wellhead did the same to Hayley's left arm, labeling these circles six, seven, eight, nine, and ten.

"Okay," Nurse Wellhead said. "We're ready. Now we have to think of things you *could* be allergic to and rub them in the little circles. First let's try peanut butter. A lot of people are allergic to peanut butter, and I've noticed a strong peanut butter smell in your room lately."

Hayley nodded. She had noticed it, too.

Nurse Wellhead went to her cupboard and found some peanut butter. She smeared a little on Hayley's skin inside the little circle labeled number one. Hayley and Nurse Wellhead waited. Nothing

happened. Hayley was glad. She didn't want to be allergic to peanut butter. She loved peanut-butter-and-jelly sandwiches.

"Let's see if you're allergic to math," Nurse Wellhead said. "Many kids and grownups are. They think they're not good at it, but really they are allergic to it."

"How will we desd id?" asked Hayley.

"That's easy!" said Nurse Wellhead. And she took the felt-tipped pen and wrote 12 + 3 x 9 - 7 in circle number two. "That ought to do it," she said. They watched Hayley's arm again. No rash.

In the third circle they rubbed some cat hairs because Hayley had noticed that her desk sometimes meowed. No rash.

In the fourth circle they rubbed some feathers because Eva was Hayley's best friend, and sometimes she had feathers stuck to her clothing. No rash.

In the fifth circle they tested boys. Nurse Wellhead grabbed a boy who was passing by and had him touch Hayley's arm in circle number five. No rash. Hayley was surprised. She thought that might be it.

In the sixth, seventh, eighth, and ninth circles Nurse Wellhead rubbed crayons, chalk, broccoli, and pencil shavings. No rash. Neither Nurse Wellhead nor Hayley had any idea what to rub in the tenth circle. Hayley had begun to lose hope. "We'll dever fide it!" she cried.

Just then Mrs. Hevelheed poked her head inside the office. She beckoned to Nurse Wellhead and said, "May I have a moment with you, please?"

Nurse Wellhead patted Hayley on the arm and went to the doorway to talk with Mrs. Hevelheed.

Hayley wished she knew what they were saying, but Mrs. Hevelheed was whispering and Hayley couldn't hear. *It must be a secret,* Hayley thought. As she craned her neck to listen, she got a sudden sneezing attack.

"ACHOO ACHOO ACHOO!" she sneezed.

"I'm sorry, Mrs. Hevelheed," said Nurse Wellhead, "but I must attend to my patient." She rushed back over to Hayley and handed her a tissue. Mrs. Hevelheed left and took her secret with her.

"Oh, you poor dear. I'm so sorry to have kept you waiting like that."

Hayley's sneezes had stopped for the moment. "Thad'z ogay, Durze Wellhead, I don'd mide sneezig doh muj. My, dere are a lod of secreds—ACHOO!—aroud thiz zgool."

"Yes, dear, I know. Wait! What did you say?"

"I said, 'My, dere are a lod of secreds—ACHOO!—aroud thiz zgool.' Oh! Durze Wellhead! I'b sneezig again, and we only hab one liddle zirgle lefd doo dry!"

"Never you mind, dear. I think I may have an idea."

"Really! Wud iz id?" asked Hayley.

"I'll whisper it to you," said Nurse Wellhead. She bent down and whispered something into the tenth little circle on Hayley's arm. Hayley couldn't hear what it was. All of a sudden she felt a terrific tingling in her arm. "Ooooooh!" she said. Nurse Wellhead and Hayley both looked at the tenth circle. It was bright red, and little bumps were starting to form. Definitely a rash.

"That's it!" said Nurse Wellhead. "You're allergic to secrets!"

"Zegreds? Bud wud cad we do aboud id?" asked Hayley.

"Unfortunately, not very much," said Nurse Wellhead. "Not yet, anyway. A doctor I know is working on a shot for people who are allergic to secrets, but it isn't nearly ready yet. I guess you will just have to switch classes. Ms. Snickle's class must have way too many secrets in it for a person with your allergy."

"Bud I cad't!" cried Hayley. "All bye freds are id thad class. Eba ad Oliber. Ad wud aboud Ms. Sdiggle? I cad't leave Ms. Sdiggle!"

Nurse Wellhead felt sorry for Hayley. Since she came to her office so often, she was one of her favorite students. Nurse Wellhead didn't want

Hayley to be unhappy. But she knew if Hayley's parents and Mrs. Hevelheed found out about the cause of Hayley's allergy, they would insist she switch classes.

"The only other choice we have is not to tell anyone that we found out what you're allergic to. Then you will keep sneezing, but at least you can stay in the class with your friends and Ms. Snickle. Is that what you want to do?"

"YEZ!" shouted Hayley.

"Are you sure?" asked Nurse Wellhead.

"I'b really, really sure!" said Hayley, nodding vigorously.

"Okay, then," said Nurse Wellhead, pulling Hayley's sleeves down to cover all the allergy-test circles. "It will be our little secret."

"ACHOO!" sneezed Hayley.

chapter eight

The Runaway Secret

"Bzzzzz," buzzed Eva's desk (which was really Ms. Snickle's alarm clock). Ms. Snickle sat up in Lacey's desk (which was really her bed), leaned over, and switched off the alarm. Sun streamed into the classroom and bounced off the desks . . . er, furniture.

"What a glorious day!" Ms. Snickle exclaimed. She got out of Lacey's desk (which was really her bed) and opened Nathan's desk (which was really her freezer). She took out a container of pineapple-pepperoni ice cream and ate straight out of the container. She put a couple of spoonfuls of ice cream into the dish on the floor and called, "Here, Shirley."

No Shirley.

She tried again. *"Here, Shirley!"*

No Shirley.

Ms. Snickle's apartment was not very big. It was, in fact, exactly the size of a classroom. This, of course, was no coincidence, since it *was* a classroom. It was not big enough to hide in for very long.

Ms. Snickle spoke loudly to Shirley, wherever she was hiding. "Shirley, it's eight o'clock. The children will be arriving at eight-forty. This is not—I repeat, *not*—a good time for you to be hiding. Now, I have left some very nice pineapple-pepperoni ice cream in your dish by Nathan's desk—I mean, the freezer—so please come out and have your breakfast before all the children arrive."

Ms. Snickle looked around.

No Shirley.

Ms. Snickle was beginning to worry. She loved Shirley very much. Shirley had black and gray markings like pencil smudges, a nose as pink as a new eraser, and eyes that gleamed like paper clips. Ms. Snickle had had Shirley since she was a kitten, small enough to fit inside a pencil box.

"Oh, dear!" Ms. Snickle exclaimed. "I do hope Shirley is all right!"

There was nothing else she could do for the

moment, so she began getting ready for school.

Ms. Snickle made her bed and watched the morning news on Dennis's desk (which was really her television set). Then she got dressed and cleaned up a bit. She threw away the empty container of pineapple-pepperoni ice cream. She did not want to leave it on someone's desk, which would be very hard to explain. Of course, if Hayley's desk wasn't there when the kids got to school . . . well, that would also be hard to explain.

"Okay, Shirley," Ms. Snickle said. "This is your last chance. It's almost time for school. Come on out and have your breakfast. In exactly *one* minute I will push the secret button."

Ms. Snickle stood next to the button and watched the clock on the wall. If Shirley was hiding when Ms. Snickle pressed the button, she would turn into Hayley's desk wherever she was, whether she was under the bed, behind the refrigerator, or in one of Ms. Snickle's shoes in the closet. (Ms. Snickle had once ruined a perfectly good shoe that way. Shirley had been hiding in it when she pressed the button. When the cat became the desk, the shoe burst all the way around! Ms. Snickle had had to press the button and turn the desk back into the cat to get it out of the closet. And she had had to buy a new pair of shoes.)

Ms. Snickle did a final check around the room for Shirley. She looked in her shoes in the closet. No Shirley. She looked under the bed. No Shirley. She looked in the freezer (you never know). No Shirley.

It was 8:40. Ms. Snickle could hear the children coming up the stairs. "Oh, well," she said to herself. "Here goes nothing." She pressed her secret button.

Instantly, the room changed. Where just a moment before there had been cozy furniture, a TV, and a coffee table, now there were neat rows of desks, except for one empty spot where Hayley's desk usually stood.

The children were now peering through the little window in the classroom door. Ms. Snickle walked over and opened it. "Good morning, children," she said. "Come sit down on the rug right away. We have something important to discuss."

"Are you going to have a baby?" Dennis asked. "In first grade my teacher had a baby and she left and we had to have a sub the whole rest of the year."

"Wow," said Oliver, "the same exact thing happened to me."

"You noodlehead! We were in the same class!" Dennis said.

"Oh . . . yeah," said Oliver.

"I'm not going to have a baby," Ms. Snickle said. "Come sit down and I'll tell you what happened."

All the children were very curious. They dumped their book bags on their desks and went straight over to the rug. Hayley tried to dump her book bag on her desk, but there was no desk there. She shrugged and dumped her bag on the floor instead.

"Children," began Ms. Snickle when they were all seated, "I am sure many of you noticed that something is missing from our classroom today."

"Oh, no!" wailed Nathan. "Our class guinea pig died!" Everyone started looking around. Sure enough, there was no sign of a guinea pig. Everyone started shouting. Eva burst into tears.

"Excu-u-u-use me!" Lacey sneered. "But we never *had* a class guinea pig."

"Oh, yeah," said Nathan. "I forgot." Eva cried a little more because she was sad they had never had one. Some of her favorite people were animals.

"What we are missing," Ms. Snickle explained, "is Hayley's desk."

"Oh!" said Hayley. "I thoughd I used doo hab a desg." Hayley's nose was stuffed up as usual. All the children looked where Hayley's desk should have been. Sure enough, there was no desk there.

"I bet it was stolen!" yelled Oliver.

"It could have been," said Ms. Snickle, "or it may have just wandered off. I may have accidentally left the window open last n—I mean, yesterday. Regardless, this is a very important matter. This city is no place for a lost ca—I mean, desk. We will simply have to go on an emergency field trip."

"YAY!" all the children yelled.

"Where will we go?" asked Dennis.

"We will go," Ms. Snickle explained, "in search of Hayley's desk."

Ms. Snickle's class prepared to go on their field trip to find her cat, Shirley . . . er, Hayley's desk.

"Remember, children, it is very important when we are outside not to talk to any dogs or pet any strangers. Do you understand?"

All the children nodded.

"When we get outside, we will look around carefully for Hayley's desk. It could be anywhere, really—chasing pigeons, lying in the sun, eating out of the garbage can. So keep your eyes peeled. Now, please line up in an orderly fashion."

The children raced to be first in line. As usual, Lacey won, tripping Dennis and Oliver when they got in her way. The children ended up in two straight lines. Everyone had a partner except Lacey. She wanted to be first all by herself, so she wouldn't be anyone's partner. That was fortunate, since no one would have wanted to be her partner, anyway.

Ms. Snickle led the class in an orderly fashion down the two flights of stairs, past Jimmy, and out onto the street. The children looked this way and that way.

"Hey!" shouted Oliver.

"What is it?" asked Ms. Snickle eagerly. "Did you find it?"

"No, but look! That's my apartment!"

Everybody looked.

"Hey, Oliver. Is that window with the red curtains *your* bedroom?"

"Yeah!" said Oliver.

"Is that barking coming from *your* dog?"

"Yeah!" said Oliver.

"Is that *your* underwear your mom is hanging out on the line to dry?"

"Uh . . . I think we should really start looking for the desk now," said Oliver.

"I quite agree," Ms. Snickle said anxiously.

"Hey, look!" shouted Lacey.

"Did you find it?" asked Ms. Snickle hopefully.

"No, but look! That's the store where *if* I don't dawdle and *if* I promise to do all of my homework first and *not* watch TV until after dinner *and* be nice to my little brother, then my mom sometimes lets me buy a piece of bubblegum."

"Oh," said Ms. Snickle politely.

"Better not let Mrs. Hevelheed see you," warned Dennis.

"Hey, look!" said Eva.

"I don't suppose you found it?" asked Ms. Snickle wearily.

"No, but I see where I live!" Eva was pointing excitedly toward the park.

"Where?" asked Hayley. "I don'd zee a building!"

Eva was about to explain that she didn't live in a building but next to the nicest little pond in the park.

But Lacey interrupted. "You don't even know

where your building is!" she said, and laughed meanly.

Eva blushed. She knew the other kids lived in apartments, but it had never occurred to her that maybe it was odd that she didn't. Before she could give it too much thought, Nathan shouted.

"Hey, look! I found it!" he cried, pointing.

Sure enough, there was Hayley's desk, looking scared and hungry. A few pencils had fallen out of it, but other than that it looked healthy, just tired from its exciting morning. Ms. Snickle came over and patted its head . . . er, top. It rubbed against her leg and made a sound almost like a purr.

"Good job, Nathan!" Ms. Snickle said. The children all gathered around excitedly. They no longer stood in an orderly fashion.

Ms. Snickle looked at all the children. *Oh, dear,* she thought. She wondered if they were all there or if some of them had gotten lost.

"How many children are in our class?" she asked.

No one knew. "Oh, well, let's go back to school. When we get to our classroom, we'll see if there is one child for each desk. If so, we'll know we have everyone."

"Unless another desk ran away," said Dennis.

"That's true," said Ms. Snickle, "but I doubt that will have happened. Line up, children."

Lacey raced to the front of the line. She tripped Hayley and Nathan along the way, but she made it there first.

Dennis, Hayley, Oliver, and Eva each took a corner of the desk and carried it back to school.

When they got to the classroom, Ms. Snickle had the children sit at their desks. There was exactly one desk for each child. All the children hugged their desks. Hayley hugged her desk the hardest.

Everyone looked tired but happy. Everyone except Eva. She just looked tired. Ms. Snickle noticed right away and took Eva aside while the other children were still hugging their desks.

"Eva, are you okay?" Ms. Snickle asked gently.

Eva shrugged. She wanted to explain, but she just didn't know how.

Ms. Snickle tried again. "Is everything okay at home?"

"Home?" said Eva. She had a faraway look. Ms. Snickle wondered if Eva had heard her.

"Yes, home . . . where you live."

"Well . . ." began Eva. She thought about the

pigeons and the ducks around the pond in the park where she lived. "Well, sometimes I just don't feel like I belong there. Sometimes I feel most at home right here."

Ms. Snickle smiled warmly and hugged her. "Me, too," she said quietly.

Over the years, Ms. Snickle had often heard her students talk this way. She herself could remember having similar feelings as a girl. But now that she was a grownup, she spent all her time at home! She looked around her apartment . . . er, classroom and chuckled to herself.

"Ms. Snickle?"

Ms. Snickle came out of her daydreams and looked seriously at Eva.

"I know it's hard, Eva, but I want you to try talking about your feelings at home. Now, promise me you will."

Eva looked up into Ms. Snickle's caring green eyes.

"I'll try," she promised.

chapter nine

Dennis's Secret

That afternoon Eva walked slowly to the park. She didn't feel quite herself. She crouched in the cool grasses and stared at the water. In the sunlight it looked almost silver. She was still there when the pigeons returned in the evening.

"What's the matter, dear?" asked one of them. She was large (for a pigeon) with dark gray stripes that sparkled in the moonlight, and she had grown to care deeply for Eva.

"I don't know," said Eva. "Sometimes I just feel so out of place, like I don't really belong. Today we went on this field trip, and the other children in my class were all pointing to their apartments and their bus stops and their candy stores, and I don't really have a place of my own." Eva felt the familiar fluttering in her heart.

"This is your place, dear," crooned the pigeon comfortingly. "You know we all love you."

"I know," said Eva, "and I really am happy here, but I feel like maybe there's a whole side of me that I don't know." Eva's secret danced around impatiently, trying to get out. "I only *wish* I knew what it was." She sighed very deeply.

It may have been because of that tiny turtle that grants big wishes, or maybe it was just the right moment, but as Eva sighed, her secret grabbed hold of it. As the sigh escaped her, so did her secret, exulting in its sudden freedom. The funny fluttering in her heart was gone. All that remained was a warm feeling.

That's just my magic, she said to herself knowingly.

Eva smiled happily at the pigeon. "Do you want to see what I learned in school?"

"Of course, dear," said the pigeon. She was always proud of Eva's accomplishments.

Eva took out a piece of paper and showed it to the pigeon. If the pigeon had been able to read, she would have known that it said: THERE IS A LITTLE FLUTTER IN MY STOMACH. I THINK IT MIGHT BE MY SECRET TRYING TO GET OUT. It was Eva's homework assignment from the first day of school. She didn't need it anymore.

The pigeon watched with great interest as Eva folded the paper this way and that. She tucked the corners, creased the folds sharply, and bent out the sides. When she was done, it looked just like a swan—an elegant swan with a long neck.

"That's beautiful!" murmured the pigeon appreciatively.

Eva walked to the edge of the water and set the swan afloat. She watched it glide gracefully away from her across the surface of the silver water.

* * *

The next day when Eva went to school, she walked a little taller. Her chin stuck out slightly, like the beak of a proud swan, which, she now knew, was exactly what she was (or used to be, anyhow). She walked gracefully up the stairs and through the doorway of the Murmer Street School. She waved hello to Jimmy, then walked up the two flights of stairs to Ms. Snickle's room.

There was a lot of commotion. Hayley had just lost a tooth.

"Let me see!" cried Oliver.

Hayley held up her tooth.

"I don't want to see the *tooth!*" cried Oliver. "I want to see the *hole* where the tooth *was!*"

Hayley opened her mouth and pointed.

"OOOOOH!" said Oliver.

"OOOOOH!" said everybody else.

"Bay I hab a yellow dreajure jest?" Hayley asked Ms. Snickle.

"Ob course—I mean, of course!" Ms. Snickle went to her desk to get it. Dennis yawned and walked away.

In Ms. Snickle's class, when you lost a tooth, you got to pick a little plastic treasure chest to keep it in so you wouldn't lose it. Then at night you would put it under your pillow and the tooth fairy would come. She would take away your tooth but leave you the treasure chest and also some money—a quarter or, if you were really lucky, maybe even a dollar.

Eva had never lost any teeth. After all, swans are birds, and birds don't even have teeth. Eva felt around in her mouth with her tongue. Teeth! They felt very good. *I wonder,* thought Eva, *if now that I'm a girl, I will start losing my teeth.* She hoped so. She tried to wiggle her front teeth with her tongue. It seemed to her that the one on the left wiggled ever so slightly. Or was it just her imagination?

"What if I'm the only kid who never loses any teeth!" cried Eva.

"Oh, don't worry about that," said Dennis. "Your teeth will fall out when they're ready. Everybody's do . . . except mine, that is. I won't ever lose *my* teeth."

"Why not?" asked Eva.

"It's genetic," Dennis explained.

"What's 'genetic' mean?" asked Oliver.

"It means 'stupid,'" said Lacey.

Dennis glared at her. "No, it doesn't," he said.

"It means it has to do with my family. People in my family don't lose their teeth. Like the way some people need glasses and some don't. If your parents need glasses, you are more likely to need them, too. In my family people don't lose their teeth."

"How awvul," said Hayley through her sniffles. "If you don'd lose ady deeth, the dooth vairy musd neber cub."

"Oh, she comes anyway," said Dennis. "The tooth fairy is my mother."

"Yeah," said Nathan, "mine, too. Mine leaves me a quarter for each tooth."

"That's it?" yelled Oliver. "Mine leaves me a dollar! Two for a molar!"

"No," explained Dennis, "the tooth fairy really *is* my mother."

"Mide is doo," said Hayley. "Id was easy doo vigure oud because she wrides a liddle node wid the money thad says 'Love, the Dooth Vairy,' and id's in my mom's handwriting."

"I saw my mom being the tooth fairy once," said Oliver. "I actually woke up and there she was!"

"WOW!" said all the other kids.

"But my mom *really* is the tooth fairy," said Dennis. No one listened except Lacey, and she only half-listened. She was staring at Dennis's perfect teeth.

Dennis walked away with his pearly white teeth. His mother really *was* the tooth fairy. Sure, every kid's mother or father took their child's tooth and replaced it with money under the pillow, but they were just helpers, like Santa's elves helping Santa Claus during the Christmas rush. Dennis's mom had the hard job. Early every morning, right at that moment when the sky is the color of old teeth, she traveled around in a flying chariot and collected every last tooth. Then she brought them all home and let Dennis keep the ones that belonged to his friends.

Sometimes Dennis worried that he was breaking the class rule, No Telling Secrets. But then he would look at his homework assignment from the first day of school. He had it hanging on the refrigerator:

DENNIS

Secrets are very tricky things. If you tell a secret, is it still a secret? Is a secret something that nobody else knows, or that most people don't know? What if you tell a secret, but nobody believes you? Then have you told a secret or not? If a tree falls in a forest and nobody hears it, does it make a noise? I don't know what that has to do with secrets, but it is an interesting question!

Dennis had given the matter much thought. In his opinion, trees *didn't* make a sound if no one heard them fall, and kind of in the same way, he figured his secret was like a tree. It wasn't telling a secret if nobody believed it was true. And if no one believed him, then he hadn't broken the rule.

Everyone was still standing around Hayley.

"Well," said Ms. Snickle. "Since everyone seems so interested in losing teeth, I have a special snack for the occasion." She walked around the room putting a crisp, shiny red apple on top of each person's desk.

Hayley's desk purred a little at the smell of food, even though it much preferred ice cream to apples. Then it went back to its usual nap.

When she got to Eva's desk, Ms. Snickle whispered to Eva, "Are things better at home?"

Eva smiled happily. "I took your advice, and I feel much better."

"That's wonderful," said Ms. Snickle, and she went to hand out the rest of the apples.

Eva bit into her apple.

"Ow!" she cried.

"What's wrong, Eva?"

"My tooth feels kind of funny." The apple was harder than she had expected. She poked at her tooth with her tongue.

"Maybe your tooth's going to fall out!" cried Oliver. "Can I see?"

All the children gathered around Eva's desk. When Eva's tooth didn't fall out, they returned to their own desks and their own apples. They spent the rest of the day biting hard into their apples. Everyone wanted their teeth to come out. They wiggled them around with their tongues and did everything they could to make them come out. But Dennis knew better. Teeth come out when they're ready, not just because you want them to.

Just before three o'clock, Eva's tooth was ready.

"My tooth!" she cried, holding it gingerly in her hand.

"COOL!" yelled Oliver. "Let me see!"

She showed him the tooth.

"No, I want to see the *hole* where the tooth *was!*"

She showed him the hole.

"COOL!"

Eva thought so, too. She chose a purple treasure

chest and carried the tooth in it very carefully. She was very excited, although she worried a bit about whether the tooth fairy—whoever she was—would find her in the park. She put the tooth under her book bag and hoped for the best.

chapter ten

Secrets Under the Moon

It was just before dawn. The moon was out, bright and round. Eva rustled in her sleep but didn't wake. If she had woken up, she might have heard the air whisper as a chariot of old teeth drifted in. But contented dreams filled her mind, and she didn't hear a thing.

In the Murmer Street School all was still, too. Ms. Snickle, no longer smelling of peanut butter or bubblegum, slept soundly in Lacey's desk. Next to her, Hayley's desk was curled up tight, dreaming of little birds and mice. Otherwise, the school was empty—except for one small mouse that had made its way inside, hoping for crumbs. The mouse had found some mango and mustard dribbles in the corner of Ms. Snickle's room. It wasn't the mouse's favorite, but it was better than nothing. It was fortunate for the mouse that Shirley was asleep, because Shirley loved mice. It was also fortunate for the mouse that Ms. Snickle was asleep, because Ms. Snickle hated mice.

At home in her bed Lacey tossed and turned, unable to sleep. Something nagged at her. It was what Dennis had said yesterday, the way he had kept insisting that his mother was the tooth fairy. Could it be true? Lacey wondered. Could she *really* be the tooth fairy? It sounded pretty silly, but then again . . . didn't Dennis have perfect teeth? And hadn't the tooth fairy been leaving her only a quarter when the other kids always got a dollar? Before, Lacey had blamed her mother, but now it all added up! It must be Dennis's mother's fault. *And* Dennis's fault. He'd probably been telling his mother to leave her less than the other kids. The more Lacey thought about it, the more sense it made. But she had to be sure. Now, what would be the best way to find out a secret for sure?

Lacey got out of bed and went to her underwear drawer. She felt around in the back until she found what she was looking for. It was her homework assignment from the first day of school. She read it over carefully:

LACEY

Secrets are very important. The most important thing about secrets is discovering them. There are many ways to do this:

1. Spy on people on their way to school.
2. Spy on people on their way home from school.
3. Spy on people during school.
4. Use technology.
5. If you're lucky, a secret might even fall into your lap.

P.S. You might be right that everyone else has secrets, but not me.

Which method should she use? Lacey read the list several times and finally decided on "Use technology." It seemed everyone was always talking about technology these days—computers and the Internet and stuff like that. Lacey quietly tiptoed downstairs and into the living room, hoping she wouldn't wake her parents or Bubba. She turned on the computer. It whirred and buzzed. She dialed up and listened for the scratchy beeping

noise that told her she was online. Then she typed WWW.TOOTHFAIRY.COM. In a few moments a page appeared that read HELLO, CHILDREN! THE TOOTH FAIRY WELCOMES YOU TO WWW.TOOTHFAIRY.COM!

Lacey started exploring the site. There was a fairy tale about a princess who lost her first tooth, and then there was a chart about how you should always brush your teeth and stay away from candy. There was also a video game in which teeth dropped from the top of the screen and you tried to catch them by moving a little pink and white cartoon tooth fairy across the bottom of the screen. Whenever you caught one, you got three points. Lacey played for a few minutes, but it was pretty boring. Then a little red button in the right-hand corner caught her eye. It was labeled GROWNUPS ONLY. Eagerly Lacey clicked on it.

Immediately a new page opened. It had no games or charts—just a letter. As Lacey read, her mouth fell open.

Dear Grownups,

I am the tooth fairy. As you may already know, in the early morning, when the sky is the color of old teeth, I travel across the world in a special chariot and collect all the children's teeth that fell out the day before, leaving special gifts in return. But I need your help!

For some time now parents in the cities have been helping me with my heavy workload. If you don't mind, when your son or daughter loses a tooth, please remove it yourself and leave it in the designated pick-up box in the lobby of your building. It's a lot easier for me to stop just once for each building rather than visit each separate apartment. When I pick up the teeth, I will leave the money in the drop-off box. If you could retrieve it before your child wakes up and leave it under your child's pillow, it would be most appreciated.

Oh! And try not to be seen! I'm sensitive about needing to use parent volunteers. I hope eventually to have a staff, the way Santa has elves to help out. My son, Dennis, is already a great helper, but he is too young to fly around on a chariot by himself. I do hope when he is older he can help me run the business, although he has aspirations of being a dentist instead.

Anyway, thanks again for your help.

The Tooth Fairy

So it was true! Lacey's eyes narrowed meanly, but then she broke into a toothy smile. She'd show Dennis! She'd think of something. She shut down the computer, tiptoed back upstairs, and fell soundly asleep. She dreamed that all of Dennis's teeth fell out, and his mother only gave him a nickel!

* * *

Just before seven o'clock Eva awoke to the cool morning. The pigeons and ducks were already up and going about their business. Eva had the feeling that something special had happened. Her tooth! She reached under her book bag, which she used as a pillow. There was her little purple treasure chest. Disappointment washed over her. The treasure chest was still there. The tooth fairy must not have come. Probably she only visited real girls—not girls who used to be swans.

Eva picked up the little chest. It felt heavy, not the way it had last night. Gingerly she undid the little latch and lifted the lid. Inside the chest were three tiny, perfect pink seashells and a silver dollar, gleaming in the morning sun. Today would be a good day.

At seven o'clock sharp Ms. Snickle's alarm clock (which was really Eva's desk) buzzed shrilly. Ms. Snickle pressed the button to turn it off and rolled over. Shirley opened one sleepy eye. A strange new smell was in the classroom. Mmm! Shirley knew that smell. Mouse! She licked her lips. Today would be a good day.

* * *

Also at seven o'clock Lacey's alarm clock (which really *was* her alarm clock) buzzed annoyingly. Lacey smacked it hard, and it stopped. She was very tired. She hadn't slept much. She climbed out of bed. She had the feeling she had dreamed something. Now, what could it be? She tried to recall the images. Teeth . . . nickels . . . Ah! She remembered now. Lacey smiled. Today would be a good day.

chapter eleven

A ~~Good~~ Bad Day for Secrets

"What *are* you doing?" Ms. Snickle asked her cat, Shirley. Ms. Snickle was getting ready to push her secret button, but Shirley kept sniffing in the corners of the room.

"Shirley, *please* get in your proper place. It's almost time for the children to arrive." Shirley made her way distractedly to her proper place. She hadn't found that mouse yet. Her mango-mustard ice cream breakfast had been good, of course, but she did have a hankering for mouse. Shirley didn't mention the mouse to Ms. Snickle. She knew how much Ms. Snickle hated mice.

Ms. Snickle pressed the button, and just in time. The chandeliers and flowered carpets flickered and vanished. The room the children entered looked just as a classroom should—tidy rows of desks, bright fluorescent lights, and bulletin boards filled with math worksheets, colorful report covers, and pencil-shaving designs. Everyone bustled about greeting one another and admiring Eva's silver dollar and pink shells. Lacey looked carefully at Eva's catch from the tooth fairy, and then she looked at Dennis. She decided she would wait for the right moment.

A small mouse poked its head out from behind the radiator, but none of the kids saw it. Hayley's desk inched a little closer to the radiator and meowed, as much as a desk can meow, which isn't much.

It was enough. The mouse jumped and then skittered across the floor.

"EEEK, A MOUSE!" screamed Ms. Snickle.

"Meow!" purred Hayley's desk.

"ACHOO!" sneezed Hayley.

Ms. Snickle was dreadfully afraid of mice. This was not a secret. Everyone knew it. Once, when she was little, a mouse had made fun of how she looked in her glasses, and ever since then she had been dreadfully afraid of them.

Whenever a mouse was in the classroom—which wasn't often, thanks to Hayley's desk—Ms.

Snickle did the same thing. She stood on top of her desk and yelled, "AAAAHHHH!" That's what she did now.

All the kids burst into action. They knew they had to get that mouse! Nathan chased it around the room, but it was too fast for him. Lacey threw her bubblegum at it, but missed. Hayley sneezed on it, which made it a little wet but didn't slow it down.

Ms. Snickle stood on top of her desk trying to be brave. Oliver threw his body at the mouse. He

missed and instead knocked into Eva's desk. Buzzing loudly, the desk slid across the room. "I've got it," Dennis called through his pearly teeth, and lunged toward it. Before he could reach it, he hit Hayley's desk, which let out a sharp meow as it twirled across the room. It knocked into another desk, which rang twice and a voice on an answering machine said, "You have reached the home of Ms. Sn—" but before the machine could finish, another desk banged into that one, and then another and another. Some mango-mustard ice cream leaked onto the floor. The mouse stopped just long enough to lick some up and then, with a loud squeak, ran out the door.

A big pile of children lay in the middle of the classroom. An even bigger pile of desks was mixed in with the pile of children. Some music came from one of the desks. A pair of fancy dress shoes stuck out of another.

I must get that button looked at, thought Ms. Snickle. *It seems to be malfunctioning a bit lately.* She climbed off her desk and blinked the lights for quiet. The pile of children lying in the middle of the floor got quiet. So did the desks.

"Thank you for chasing away the mouse," said

Ms. Snickle. "I do have such a dreadful fear of them ever since that incident when I was just a little girl—*sniff*. Anyway, please get up gently and put your desks back where they go. It is very important that they get back in *exactly* the right places. It is VERY, VERY IMPORTANT!"

The children did not know why it was so important, but they listened to Ms. Snickle and they tried their best to put the desks back the way they were. They slid them and pushed them and lifted them and twirled them and pulled them and heaved them and nudged them and pleaded with them. It's funny how it takes a lot more effort to clean a room than to mess it up. It was slow going, and they were just about to do a final check to make sure all the desks were in *exactly* the right places when someone knocked on the door.

It was Nurse Wellhead.

"Hi, Hayley, how are those sniffles?" Nurse Wellhead asked, winking.

"I'b ogay," Hayley replied, sniffling and winking back.

"Ms. Snickle," the nurse said in a loud whisper that every curious child could easily hear. "By accident I received a triple order of cough drops. If your students are interested, you could send them to my office to get some."

"Why, thank you!" said Ms. Snickle. "I am sure they will all be very interested. As soon as they are done moving these desks we'll . . . Where did they go?"

Ms. Snickle looked around. There were no children. Thankfully, there were also no mice. There were what looked like perfectly arranged desks in orderly rows across the room.

"Well," said Ms. Snickle. "I guess they have already gone for the cough drops. I do hope the desks are in the right places . . ."

Lacey was sucking on her fourth cherry cough drop when the right moment came along. She cornered Dennis outside the nurse's office. He was sitting on a bench, waiting for the others to finish their cough drops. He had told Nurse Wellhead, "No, thank you." His mother didn't approve of sugary candy and cough drops.

"I know your secret," Lacey said meanly. "The tooth fairy really *is* your mother."

"Yeah, so what?" said Dennis. "It's not a secret. I told everyone yesterday. You just didn't believe me."

"Well, you're breaking our classroom rule," said Lacey.

"No, I'm not!" insisted Dennis confidently. He had already thought about it, and he knew he wasn't breaking the rule.

"Sure you are. The rule is No Telling Secrets. Well, this certainly *is* a secret. No other child in the whole *world* knows who the tooth fairy is—just you. And yesterday I heard you *telling* it to everyone, so. . . ." Lacey said triumphantly, "You *are* breaking the rule. I wonder what Ms. Snickle will do to you when she finds out!"

Dennis was confused. Something about what Lacey was saying didn't sound quite right, but he wasn't sure what it was. He wished he had his homework assignment from the first day of school with him, but he didn't. Dennis always followed the rules, and since it was *home*work, he always kept it at home. He tried to recall what it said.

"Think about it like this, Lacey," he began, trying to explain. "If a tree fell in a forest, and nobody heard it, would it make a noise?"

"If it fell on your head, it would," said Lacey. She flashed her teeth at him.

"Oh, come on," he begged. "Please don't tell Ms.

Snickle!" Dennis didn't want anyone to be mad at him—especially Ms. Snickle!

"I won't," she promised.

Dennis breathed a sigh of relief.

Lacey skipped over to where the other kids were. "Hey, guys, guess what?" Within four minutes everyone in Ms. Snickle's class knew that Dennis's mom really *was* the tooth fairy. Dennis felt awful. Some of his friends were mad at him because they only got quarters from the tooth fairy when everyone else always got a dollar. Others were angry that he had been keeping such a big secret from them. But they stopped talking about it when they got back to Ms. Snickle's room.

Ms. Snickle watched her class file quietly into the classroom. Something seemed different. Sure, all the kids smelled like cherry cough drops, but there was something else, too. She couldn't quite put her finger on what it was.

That afternoon, just before four o'clock, Ms. Snickle returned to her classroom with two pints of apricot-anchovy ice cream. She put the ice cream into Nathan's desk (or what she thought was Nathan's desk). She lay down on Oliver's desk (or what she thought was Oliver's desk) and flipped on

Dennis's desk (or what she thought was Dennis's desk).

Then she pressed her secret button.

Something didn't seem quite right. Ms. Snickle's legs felt a little cold. She looked down at her couch. It wasn't her couch! She was lying on Nathan's desk (which was really her freezer) and she was getting freezed! She had turned on Hayley's desk (which was really her cat, Shirley), and since Shirley had been sleeping, she did not much appreciate being turned on. Ms. Snickle had put her ice cream away in Lacey's desk (which was really her bed), and the ice cream was dripping all over her orange-flowered pillows. Her alarm clock was buzzing and the time read half-past Shirley.

"Oh, no!" said Ms. Snickle. "The children have put all the desks away in the wrong places!" Her bed was standing on its side where her refrigerator usually stood. Her microwave was meowing and chewing on a piece of cat food. And her coffee table was ringing. It rang twice and a voice said, "You have reached the coffee table of Ms. Snickle. I can't come—" Ms. Snickle picked up her coffee table. "Hello?" she said into one of the legs. "Hello?"

"Oh," said a voice. "I must have the wrong number. I was trying to reach Ms. Snickle's telephone, not her coffee table. Bye." Click. Ms. Snickle put down her coffee table leg. She did not know what to do. She was much too tired to move all her furniture. The children would have to do that tomorrow.

She felt inside her pillowcase and found a container of apricot-anchovy ice cream. She took a spoon out of her bathtub and ate the whole container. Then she drank some water from her telephone and climbed into her alarm clock. "Good night, Shirley," she said to her microwave oven. She turned off her couch and went to sleep.

She dreamed of mice wearing glasses being chased by microwave ovens that purred and ate ice cream. In her sleep she brushed some crunchy anchovy bits out of her hair.

chapter twelve

"I Know a Secret"

The next day Lacey left for school smiling. Discovering Dennis's secret had taken a lot of work, but it had been worth it just to see the look on his face. It had been even more exciting when everyone started yelling at him.

Lacey reached into her pocket and pulled out a piece of bubblegum and a piece of paper. She popped the gum into her mouth and opened up the paper. It was her list of ways to discover secrets. She had decided to carry it with her all the time. She looked at number one: *Spy on people on their way to school.* Perfect! Here she was on the way to school, and if she waited long enough, she was sure to see someone good to spy on. Lacey hid against a building and waited.

Before long, Nathan and his disgusting little sister, Suzy, walked by. *Ew,* thought Lacey, but she followed them anyway.

Spying was trickier than she had expected. She had to stay far enough behind so that they couldn't see her, but if she was too far behind, she couldn't hear what they were saying. Then Nathan and Suzy came to a crosswalk. There was a red light and they had to wait. Lacey made her move. She hid behind a large tree right near them and listened.

"I love you," Nathan said to his little sister, patting her on the head.

"I love you, too," she said back.

"EWWWW!" cried Lacey. It's a good thing the ew-meter wasn't there, or it might have broken again.

Nathan and Suzy heard Lacey and turned around.

"That is SO gross!" said Lacey. "I can't believe it!"

Nathan turned white. "P-p-please don't tell," he whispered.

"Why shouldn't I?" Lacey asked. She was over the initial shock now and was beginning to enjoy it.

"You'd be breaking the class rule," said Nathan, "No Telling Secrets."

"Oh, don't worry about that, Nathan!" said

Lacey. "After I tell it, it won't be a secret anymore!" Lacey made a loud kissy noise and skipped on ahead to school. She thought it would be nice to tell the others right away, so the information could really sink in before Nathan arrived.

The third secret was much easier for Lacey to discover. It fell right into her lap. It happened during a lesson on making paper airplanes. Ms. Snickle was surprised how few children knew how to make really fast paper airplanes. As their teacher, she felt it was her duty to teach them.

The room looked like a crazy airport. Paper planes whizzed by heads and nose-dived into desks. Hundreds of planes littered the floor.

Oliver was out of paper. He reached into his pocket and was happy to find a piece. Without even looking at it, he folded it up and let it fly.

It hit Lacey square in the nose, and she fell onto her knees.

"Ow!" she cried. She picked it up, intending to rip it to shreds, when something caught her eye. The word "secret" was on the paper. She unfolded it:

OLIVER

I have a secret. You probably already know that, because you seem to know a lot about secrets. Last night I was so nervous about school that I wet my bed. Since our class rule is No Telling Secrets, I know you won't tell anyone my secret. I can see that you really understand about secrets.

Lacey grinned. It was the paper Oliver had written on the first day of school. What an awful secret! She couldn't wait to tell it.

She pulled her list out of her pocket. She had already checked off number one and number four. Now she checked off number five, *If you're lucky, a secret might even fall into your lap.* That left two more ways she hadn't tried yet. Of course, she could always use numbers one, four, and five again, but she thought it might be nice to try different methods. Since she was in school, she decided to try number three next: *Spy on people during school.* Now, whom should she spy on? She looked around the room.

"ACHOO!" sneezed Hayley.

Lacey smiled. She had found her next target.

Hayley's secret—and all the other kids' secrets—were surprisingly easy for Lacey to discover. It was just a matter of paying attention and knowing what to look for. To discover Hayley's secret, Lacey simply listened outside Nurse Wellhead's door the next time Hayley was there. Inside, Hayley and the nurse were chatting away about Hayley's allergy.

Allergic to secrets? Lacey had never heard of such a thing. It sounded pretty funny. Lacey wondered if telling Hayley's secret would make Hayley's allergy *stronger*—because then everyone would know it—or *less* strong—because then it wouldn't be a secret anymore? Less strong, she thought, but she wasn't sure. She shrugged. She decided not to give it too much thought. She'd find out soon enough when she told everyone. She checked off number three on her list.

In Lacey's opinion, Eva's secret was the weirdest one yet. She had tried to follow Eva home after school (number two: *Spy on people on their way home from school*) and instead found herself next to a pond in the park. From behind a rock Lacey watched Eva greet the pigeons and ducks as if they were family and then start a rousing game of duck, duck, pigeon. (Duck, duck, pigeon is very much like duck, duck, goose. It's the version to play if you ever find yourself with plenty of ducks and pigeons but no geese.)

After a few rounds, a large pigeon winked at Eva and said, "Maybe we should play duck, duck, swan now."

All of the older birds laughed at the joke.

"Why?" asked a little duckling who was only a few weeks old.

Smiling, Eva explained. "You see, dear, it all happened before you were born. Once upon a time I used to be a swan in a magical forest, but then an evil sorcerer changed me into a little girl, so now I go to the Murmer Street School, and live here." She smiled at the pigeon who had winked at her. "And I couldn't be happier," she finished.

Lacey stared at Eva. A swan? She looked at Eva's long white neck and proud nose. She wondered if she should have seen it all along. But Lacey knew by now that you see things better when you are looking for them.

She shook her head in amazement and walked slowly home. Finding out secrets was very exciting. She checked off number two from her list.

By Friday, Lacey had learned all of the kids' secrets and told them, of course—after all, it wouldn't be fair to keep them all to herself, would it?

Oliver laughed at Eva for having been a swan and sleeping with pigeons in the park.

"Oh, yeah, at least I don't wet my nest—I mean, bed!" said Eva, and fluttered angrily away.

Hayley teased Nathan about his sister.

"You're one to talk—Sneezy-Face!" Nathan said back.

Every day the children got grouchier and grouchier. They teased each other and called each other names like Featherhead, Blabbermouth, and

Sneezy-Face. Actually, Hayley was surprised that she was still sneezing and sniffling. If all the secrets were out in the open, then they weren't really secrets anymore and there wasn't anything for her to be allergic to.

Lacey thought of that, too, and it made her wonder. Could there be some undiscovered secret left in Ms. Snickle's class? Lacey smiled to herself contentedly. This was the most fun she had ever had in school.

By now all the children were unhappy and grouchy. Nobody got along with anyone. Everyone yelled and made angry faces, except for Ms. Snickle. She wasn't angry, but she was worried.

Ms. Snickle held a class meeting. "I am very worried about you," she said. "You used to be such happy children, but lately you seem so angry and upset. Does anyone want to talk about what is going on?"

Hayley's hand went up, just a little. Lacey looked at Hayley and mouthed, "No telling secrets." Hayley put her hand down. Would telling Ms. Snickle what happened be breaking the class rule? She wasn't sure, but she didn't want to take the chance.

"We're okay," Lacey said to Ms. Snickle, smiling brightly.

"Well, if you're sure," Ms. Snickle said.

"Oh, yes. We're sure," Lacey said. Ms. Snickle smiled and brushed some pencil shavings out of her hair. As Lacey looked at her, she had a strange idea. *I wonder,* she thought, *if Ms. Snickle has a secret, too.*

Lacey thought about it during the fractions lesson.

She thought about it during the pogo-stick lesson.

She thought about it during the juggling lesson.

By the end of the day she had a plan.

chapter thirteen

The Last Secret

It was 3:10 p.m. All the children had packed their book bags and left the classroom. Some of them went straight home. Some of them went to their cello lessons. Eva went to the park. Lacey waited outside the school behind a bush.

At 3:27, Ms. Snickle picked up her purse and left the classroom. She walked down the two flights of stairs, waved good-bye to Jimmy, and walked down the front steps of the school.

Lacey peeked out from behind her bush and saw Ms. Snickle leave. She followed her from a little distance back.

Ms. Snickle did not go home. Instead, she walked to the supermarket. Lacey walked to the supermarket, too, careful not to be seen. Ms. Snickle picked out two pints of caramel-carrot ice cream and some broccoli. Lacey stared in disbelief. Broccoli? Yuck!

Lacey watched Ms. Snickle pay for her groceries and leave. Lacey was getting excited. She couldn't wait to see where Ms. Snickle lived. Maybe that would help her learn her secret.

To Lacey's surprise Ms. Snickle walked back to school. All the children were gone now and the front door was gated shut. Ms. Snickle went in through the basement. Lacey watched from a distance.

She must have forgotten something, Lacey thought. *I'll just wait here until she comes out.*

But after twenty minutes Ms. Snickle hadn't come out.

That's strange, Lacey thought. She tried the basement entrance Ms. Snickle had used, but it was locked.

Lacey didn't know what to do next. She leaned against a tree and thought. She *had* to know what Ms. Snickle was doing inside the school. But how? All of a sudden she felt something on her head. She looked up. A pigeon was right above her, looking down with a mocking smile.

"EWWW!" Lacey cried as she wiped off her

head with a tissue. (If the ew-meter had been there, it would have registered at least a seven.)

"You must be a friend of Eva's. I'll get you for this!" Lacey put down her book bag and began to climb the tree. The pigeon watched quietly until Lacey was just about to reach its branch. Then it calmly flew away.

Lacey sat on the branch and caught her breath. When she looked up, she smiled. She hadn't gotten the pigeon, but at least she had a good view of Ms. Snickle's classroom window. She peered inside.

The light was on. The room looked the same as always, but Lacey couldn't see Ms. Snickle anywhere. *Maybe she's not in there,* Lacey thought. *Then again, I can't see the whole room. Maybe Ms. Snickle is just hidden behind something or happens to be standing where I can't see her.*

What Lacey saw next almost made her fall out of the tree. A strange light suddenly shimmered in the classroom, the desks flickered and then vanished. In their place was a couch and a coffee table and a telephone. There was a bed with orange-flowered pillows. A beautiful carpet covered the floor. Oil paintings in fancy gold frames hung on the walls, and crystal chandeliers hung

from the ceiling. A television set glowed brightly in the middle of the room.

Where was Lacey's desk? Where were all of the other desks? Where were the fluorescent lights? The bulletin boards? The math worksheets and colorful report covers? And what was that black and gray cat doing there?

Lacey was a clever girl. She thought about what she saw and reached a logical conclusion. *She must have pressed a secret button,* Lacey thought knowingly. *I only wish I knew where it was.*

Lacey couldn't believe her luck. This secret was even better than she could ever have imagined. It was better than Sneezy-Face and Goody Tooth Shoes and Featherhead. But she had to handle it properly. This was too important to share with the other children. No. An important secret like this had to be told to . . . an important person.

chapter fourteen

A Secret Note

Lacey sat at her desk at home with a piece of fancy stationery in front of her. She wrote the note carefully. She used her best handwriting and rechecked her spelling. She wanted to make sure the principal took the note seriously.

The next day at school Lacey slipped it under the principal's door. Then she went to class and waited.

Now, principals often receive strange notes. Parents send notes that the math is too hard, the books are too easy, the teachers are too old, and the food is too salty. Teachers send notes that the school year is too long, the children are too short, the food is too soggy, and the chalk is too squeaky. Students send notes that the vacations are too short, the homework is too long, the teachers are too mean, and the food is too healthy.

Mrs. Hevelheed read these notes every day from 10:00 a.m. to 10:05 a.m. After she read them, she put them in a special drawer. It had a big hole in the bottom and was right over her wastebasket. She had found this to be a very efficient system for filing her important correspondence. It was 10:02 when she got to Lacey's note:

Dear Mrs. Hevelheed,

I am in Ms. Snickle's class and I just wanted to let you know that I found out a secret about Ms. Snickle. At night, when we all go home, she uses a secret button to turn the classroom into her apartment. She sleeps in school . . . and she eats too much ice cream!

Sincerely,

A concerned student

Mrs. Hevelheed began to put the note in the drawer with the big hole in it, but then she thought, *Hmm, this one is a little different.*

The part about ice cream had gotten her attention. It was not appropriate for a teacher to eat ice cream. It was only slightly better than chewing gum. Mrs. Hevelheed herself never ate ice cream. She ate only turnips and moldy bread.

Mrs. Hevelheed filed the rest of the notes in the drawer with the hole over the wastebasket without even reading them. She took a large book off the shelf. It was called *The Official Principal Handbook.* She turned to Chapter 13, "Reasons for Firing a Teacher." She skimmed quickly. Nothing about ice cream. Amazing! She had thought that alone would be enough reason to fire a teacher. Then she saw something else. Reason number 37: "A principal may fire a teacher for staying overnight in school without permission." Mrs. Hevelheed called for her secretary.

"Would you send for Ms. Snickle, please."

Ms. Snickle's class was having a spelling zee. Other classes have spelling bees, but Ms. Snickle's class was more advanced. A spelling zee is like a spelling bee except all the words have a *z* in them. (Sometimes Ms. Snickle's class even had spelling whys, where you had to explain *why* you would ever want to spell the word. With some words, this could be quite a challenge.)

In today's spelling zee, Lacey had lost right away. She had spelled zoo with two *z*'s and one *o*, instead of the other way around. Her mind just wasn't on her work. She was too excited. It was Eva's turn. Her word was *zigzag*. "Z-i-g," she began. She had spelled *zig* correctly, but she would never get to *zag*, for just then the door opened and the secretary popped her head in.

"Ms. Snickle, Mrs. Hevelheed needs to see you right away."

Lacey smiled to herself. *The fun has begun!* she thought.

Ms. Snickle did not come back to the classroom that day. The children weren't really worried about her. They were still too grouchy to be worried. They spent the day fighting.

"Hey, Goody Tooth Shoes, your mom only gave me a nickel for my tooth last night," Nathan told Dennis.

"What did you do with the nickel," asked Dennis, "give it to your sister?"

Everybody laughed.

"Hey, Featherhead," Lacey said to Eva, "want a nice juicy worm?"

"Don'd mage fud of her!" said Hayley.

"Hayley," said Lacey, "I have a *secret!*"

"ACHOO!" sneezed Hayley.

* * *

At 3:10 the children dismissed themselves. Eva walked to the park, but not very happily. Several children played poorly during their cello lessons. Lacey climbed the tree outside school and watched the classroom window. She was waiting for Ms. Snickle to come back. She was sure she would. Lacey figured Mrs. Hevelheed had probably made Ms. Snickle write a thousand times "I won't live in school" or something like that, but then Ms. Snickle would come back.

Lacey waited a long time. Finally she saw the lights go on in the classroom. But the person in the classroom was not Ms. Snickle. It was Mrs. Hevelheed. She was walking around the classroom, feeling the walls.

"She must be looking for the secret button," Lacey said. A pigeon on a nearby branch looked at her. "I'm not talking to you," Lacey said to the pigeon, disgusted. Only Eva talked to birds.

Mrs. Hevelheed felt all around but found nothing. After a few minutes, she turned off the light and left. Lacey stayed in the tree a while longer waiting for Ms. Snickle to come back. When it got dark, she climbed down and went home.

chapter fifteen

Telling Secrets

The next day there was a new teacher in Ms. Snickle's class.

"Good morning," the new teacher said in a voice that made it clear she didn't care if anyone had a good morning or not.

"Where's Ms. Snickle?" Oliver asked.

"She got fired," the new teacher said. "Look, I don't much care for children and I have a headache, so just keep quiet and play among yourselves." The new teacher took two aspirin and leaned back in Ms. Snickle's chair to take a nap. She hadn't even bothered to write her name on the board.

The children were so stunned that at first no one said anything. Then they began to argue in low voices.

"It's *your* fault, Featherhead," Dennis said to

Eva. "Mrs. Hevelheed probably found out you talk to pigeons."

"They wouldn't fire a teacher for that," Eva said. "She probably got fired because *you're* so stupid! Sometimes teachers get blamed for things like that, you know."

The only child who remained silent was Lacey. She was confused. She ought to be happy. She had gotten Ms. Snickle in big trouble. Wasn't that what she had wanted? So why wasn't she happy?

The new teacher slept. The children argued in whispers all morning.

At noon the children took out their lunches. They were careful not to rustle their paper bags too loudly. They didn't want to wake the new teacher. At the smell of food Hayley's desk began to meow. It hadn't been fed since yesterday. Lacey felt sorry for it. She gave it some of her yogurt.

The children were all argued out. They ate without talking. Everyone felt miserable. Lacey felt the most miserable of all.

In the middle of her ham sandwich Lacey stopped eating. She put the sandwich down.

"I know a secret," said Lacey.

Nobody looked at her. Everyone had heard

that before. "It's about Ms. Snickle," she said. Now everybody looked at her.

Lacey told the other kids the story of what happened. She didn't leave anything out. She told them about spying on Ms. Snickle and what she had seen through the window and about writing the note to Mrs. Hevelheed. When she got done, the children were excited and full of questions.

"You mean our desks turn into her furniture?" asked Oliver.

"That's right," said Lacey matter-of-factly.

"So that's why Ms. Snickle always has pencil shavings in her hair!" said Dennis, peeking inside Lacey's messy desk.

"Ad thad's why my desg iz zo cuddly," said Hayley as she petted it. The desk purred a little, but not too happily. She missed Ms. Snickle too much.

Nathan sniffed his desk. It smelled like caramel and carrots. "My desk must be the freezer," he said knowingly. It did feel a little cold around the edges.

"But how does she do it?" asked Eva. "Where's the secret button?"

"That's the part I didn't see," Lacey explained. "I know there must be a secret button, but I don't know where it is."

All the kids began searching for it on the floor and the walls.

"I think I found it!" cried Oliver. Everyone came running over, but it was only a chunk of carrot that had gotten dried onto the floor.

Eva burst into tears. "I don't care where the button is!" she cried. "I just want Ms. Snickle back." Slowly the other children went back to their desks. They felt that way, too.

"Look," said Dennis loudly. "Let's not just sit here complaining about it. Let's *do* something!"

The new teacher woke up. "Can't you kids keep it down?" she said. Then she went back to sleep.

All the children put their juice box straws into a pile. Dennis cut two of them so they were shorter than the rest. Then each child picked one. Lacey and Nathan picked the two shortest straws. They would be the ones to go see Mrs. Hevelheed. Lacey spit out her gum before they went. She meant business.

Lacey had never been inside Mrs. Hevelheed's office before. Neither had Nathan, but he pretended he had. He told Lacey about it on the way there. "She keeps a tank full of snakes," he explained. "And if you're bad, she makes you stick your hand in the tank. Sometimes none of the snakes are hungry. But sometimes they are very hungry. Sometimes she forgets to feed them. Sometimes she forgets on purpose."

Lacey ignored him.

"I bet she'll smell the gum on you," Nathan went on. "She can tell if a person is even thinking about chewing gum. That's enough right there. Just thinking about it is enough."

"Save it for your sister!" Lacey said. They had reached the door now. It was closed, but they peered in through the window in the door.

On the wall was a big poster that said NO GUM. Lacey swallowed nervously and tried to smell her own breath. Nathan knocked. Mrs. Hevelheed came to the door with a huge smile on her face. Neither Nathan nor Lacey had ever seen her smile before. It was scary.

"Oh, hello, children," she said brightly. "You are, or I should say, *were*, in Ms. Snickle's class, right? How are you enjoying your new teacher?" She laughed.

"Well," said Lacey. "That's what we came to talk to you about. We want Ms. Snickle to come back."

"Oh," said Mrs. Hevelheed. "I'm afraid that's impossible. But anyway, that's none of my concern. You see, I, too, am leaving."

"Were you fired, too?" Nathan asked.

"No, but I've accepted a position with APDAG—the Association of Principals and Dentists Against Gum—in its effort to rid the entire world of gum. It's an opportunity I really couldn't turn down, you see."

Nathan and Lacey saw.

They watched Mrs. Hevelheed leave. She took her No Gum poster with her. She walked out of the building and down the street, away from the Murmer Street School. On the way back to the classroom Lacey popped a new piece of bubblegum into her mouth.

"Did I ever tell you," she asked Nathan, "how secrets are like bubblegum?"

chapter sixteen

The Proper Place for Secrets

Back in the classroom Nathan and Lacey reported to the other children, but they did it quietly so as not to wake the new teacher.

Then Lacey said, "I think we need to go on another field trip—this time to find Ms. Snickle!"

Hayley asked, "How cub you care zo buch aboud Ms. Sdiggle dow?"

"Look, Sneezy-Face," Lacey said. "Do you want to find Ms. Snickle or not?"

Everyone did. Quietly the children got their coats and lined up at the door with a partner. That's what you do when you go on a field trip. They wanted to make Ms. Snickle proud, even if she wasn't there to see them. Lacey led the way. Quietly the children walked downstairs and out of the building. They were in such a nice, orderly line that no one noticed there was no teacher with them—not even Jimmy.

The children didn't know which way to go. They started arguing all over again—this time loudly.

"I think we should look in the supermarket," Oliver said. "I mean, that's where Lacey saw her go."

"So you think she moved to the supermarket, Puddle Boy?" asked Nathan. "That doesn't make any sense. She must be *staying* somewhere."

"So where do you think we should look?"

"I don't know!"

"Well, neither do I!"

As they were yelling, a pigeon flew down and alighted on Lacey's shoulder.

Lacey recognized it. "Hey! Get this thing off me!" she shouted.

"Quiet down," Eva said. "It's trying to tell me something."

The pigeon cooed and cocked its head.

Eva nodded. Then the pigeon flew away.

"I know where Ms. Snickle is," Eva said.

"Well, tell us!" the children all shouted.

Eva pointed up. Ms. Snickle was asleep in the

tree right next to them. It was the tree just outside their classroom window.

"A lot of teachers seem to be asleep today," said Lacey, but she was glad to see Ms. Snickle.

"MS. SNICKLE!" all the children yelled.

"Oh, good morning," she said waking up. "Are you going on another field trip?"

Ms. Snickle climbed down from the tree and hugged the children. "How are you?" she asked them. "And how is Hayley's desk?"

"We fed it a little yogurt, but we didn't have any ice cream," the children explained.

Ms. Snickle was shocked. "How ever did you know?" she asked.

All the children were embarrassed. It felt funny to know their teacher's secret. Lacey was the most embarrassed of all.

Lacey explained while they walked with Ms. Snickle to the supermarket to get some ice cream for Hayley's desk. She told Ms. Snickle about Dennis's secret and about Nathan's secret. She told her about Eva's secret and about Hayley's secret.

"So that explains all the sneezing," Ms. Snickle said.

They had reached the supermarket. Ms. Snickle

picked out ten pints of broccoli-banana ice cream, so there would be enough for all the children as well as for Shirley and herself.

"Ew!" the children said as politely as they could.

"Broccoli is very good for you," Ms. Snickle explained. "You should try to eat some every day." Ms. Snickle paid for the ice cream and they all walked back toward school.

Lacey continued her explanation. She told Ms. Snickle how she had stayed after school to spy on her and about the note to Mrs. Hevelheed.

All the children watched Ms. Snickle to see what she would do. When Lacey finished the story, Ms. Snickle looked sad.

"Well, it was bound to happen," Ms. Snickle said. "I was one of the last few."

"The last few what?" Lacey asked.

"The last few teachers to live in school," Ms. Snickle said. "It used to be that all teachers lived in their classrooms. All schools were built with secret buttons that turned the desks into furniture, the fluorescent lights into chandeliers, and the bulletin boards into paintings. But it was always a secret, of course. Anything that magical has to be a secret. Don't you agree, Eva?"

Eva nodded.

"And over time," Ms. Snickle said, "more and more teachers had to leave their magical classroom-apartments every night and find other places to live."

"Do all teachers live in trees, like you?"

Ms. Snickle laughed. "Of course not. I wasn't living in that tree. I was just waiting to figure out how to get Shirley, my cat. I was very worried about her. Then I was going to find a regular apartment and try to get another job as a teacher."

"But you can't leave!" the children shouted.

By now the field trip was over. Ms. Snickle's class was back at the entrance of the Murmer Street School.

"Hello, Jimmy," Ms. Snickle said as they walked in.

"Hello, Ms. Snickle."

Ms. Snickle and her class walked up the stairs to the third floor and turned right toward Ms. Snickle's classroom.

"But what about the new teacher?" Oliver asked.

"What new teacher?" Ms. Snickle asked. The children realized they had forgotten to tell her that part. But when they walked in, the room was empty.

"New teacher!" they shouted. No one answered. She was nowhere to be found.

"Don't you know her name?" Ms. Snickle asked.

"No," the children said. "She never wrote it on the chalkboard."

"Well, she doesn't sound like much of a teacher."

Finally, Hayley found a note. It was taped to Ms. Snickle's desk. Hayley read it aloud: "Since dere are doh childred add doh prinzibul, I figure dere cad alzo be doh deacher. Good-bye."

Everyone cheered and took their seats.

Ms. Snickle dished out the ice cream and put a lot into Hayley's desk, which lapped it up quickly and purred a great deal.

When they were done eating the ice cream, Ms. Snickle looked at the clock and announced it was time for their pogo-stick lesson. Usually the children liked their pogo-stick lesson, but today everyone groaned.

"Show us your secret button!" the children cried. "We want to see the room change!"

"Oh, dear," Ms. Snickle said. "I was afraid this would happen."

"What do you mean?" Lacey asked.

"Well, I really *can't* show you. It's meant to be a secret. You shouldn't even know about it in the first place."

"Oh, come on. *Please,*" the children begged.

"I'm afraid you don't understand," Ms. Snickle said. "Think about it. How will I be able to teach you if you feel as though you're sitting in my living room all the time, and if you stop in the middle of lessons to play with Hayley's desk, and if you spend the whole day turning the fluorescent lights into chandeliers?"

Nathan and Oliver, who had been feeling around the walls for the secret button, stopped and listened.

"Some secrets must stay secret forever," Ms. Snickle said kindly but firmly.

"I wish *my* secret had been kept private," said Eva. "It's hard to be a girl when everyone keeps acting like I'm a swan." Indeed, it was true. Eva had been looking a bit feathery the past few days, ever since the other kids had found out her secret.

"Yes," Ms. Snickle agreed. "Some secrets are meant to be secret, and if a secret isn't a secret, then it isn't a secret."

Everyone nodded. It made perfect sense.

"I wish *my* secret had been kept a secret, too," Dennis said. "Then everyone wouldn't blame me for how much tooth-fairy money they get."

"I wish nobody knew *my* secret, either," Nathan said. "It's nobody else's business if I like my little sister."

"It seems that everyone has a secret," Ms. Snickle said.

"Not Lacey," said Oliver.

"Yes, even Lacey," said Ms. Snickle.

"Really?" all the children asked, including Lacey.

"Yes, really," Ms. Snickle said.

Lacey blushed.

"Thad muzd be why I'b sdill sduvd ub!" exclaimed Hayley.

"I think," said Ms. Snickle, "that out of all the secrets, Lacey's is the only one that really should have been told in the first place."

"What is it?" the children all asked.

"Lacey's secret," said Ms. Snickle, "is that she is really a very nice person."

The other children were shocked. It was the most surprising of all the secrets. But as they thought about it, they saw that it made sense. After all, hadn't Lacey gone to a lot of trouble to find Ms.

Snickle and bring her back to school? And hadn't Lacey felt very bad about all the trouble she caused?

"I wish we could forget all the secrets!" said Eva.

"Except Lacey's," added Hayley. "We shouldn't forget hers."

"Hey!" said Nathan. "You're not stuffed up anymore!" It was true. Lacey's was the last secret. There was nothing for Hayley to be allergic to anymore.

"That's it!" said Ms. Snickle. "Instead of learning to remember things this afternoon, we will learn to forget. Then they will go back to being our own secrets, as they should be. Why didn't I think of this sooner?"

"Now, gather round my desk, please," said Ms. Snickle, "and we will begin the forgetting."

Ms. Snickle collected all the children's books that had words and stories and information in them and put them away. She held up a blank book.

"What's that for?" the children asked. They looked at the pages. All the pages were the same. Empty.

"This book is where the secrets will go when we

forget them. Right now they are in our heads. When we take them out of our heads, they will have to go somewhere else, so we will put them into this book. Do you understand?"

All the children nodded.

Ms. Snickle began the lesson.

"Forgetting," she explained, "can be just as important as remembering and is often much harder to do. Has anyone ever forgotten anything before?"

Nathan raised his hand.

"Yes, Nathan."

"I forgot something once," Nathan said, "but I don't remember what it was."

All the children laughed.

"You see," Ms. Snickle said, "that is what is so hard about forgetting."

Hayley raised her hand.

"Yes, Hayley."

"I once forgot how to spell 'Mississippi,'" Hayley said clearly, with no sniffles.

"How did you do it?" Ms. Snickle asked.

"Well, I just didn't think about it, and the letters kind of left my head."

"Good!" said Ms. Snickle. "That's part of the

technique. But there is more. Now, watch carefully."

Ms. Snickle drew diagrams on the blackboard and pointed as she explained. She pulled down a chart of the human brain and showed the children exactly how forgetting works. Luckily, Ms. Snickle had taken a class in college on forgetting. At least she thought she had. She couldn't remember for sure.

The forgetting took a long time. It was a bit like unreading, or reading inside out. The children forgot one secret at a time, being careful not to forget their own secrets or Lacey's. As each secret was forgotten, it entered the blank book as a different chapter. They began with Eva's secret, because it was so easy to get into a book. It was just like a fairy tale. Then they forgot all the other secrets, including Ms. Snickle's. That was the hardest because the children really didn't want to let it go.

It took three hours to finish putting all the secrets into the book. The children were exhausted, so Ms. Snickle handed out more helpings of broccoli-bubblegum ice cream and gave them free time to relax. Everyone had worked very hard.

Nathan picked up the book of secrets and began to open it.

"Don't open it!" Ms. Snickle warned, "or all the secrets will escape and we will have to forget them all over again." Nathan quickly shut the book.

"But what will we do with the book?" Lacey asked. "Should we throw it away?"

"Oh, no," said Ms. Snickle. "Books are precious. You should never throw them away."

"But where should we put it?" asked Nathan.

"In the library, of course," said Ms. Snickle.

"The library?" all the kids asked in amazement.

"But if we put it in the library, someone might read it and learn all our secrets," said Oliver. He thought of his own secret. If he hadn't written it down, Lacey wouldn't have discovered it.

"Oh. That's a good point," said Ms. Snickle.

"I know!" said Dennis. "We can put it on the top shelf. No one ever reads the books on the top shelf. Even the librarian can't reach up there."

Everyone liked that idea, but some of the children were still worried.

"What if someone *someday* was to read it? What if that person found out all this stuff about us?"

"I've got it!" Ms. Snickle said. She got a little

label out of her desk. It was the kind library books have telling what section they belong in. Ms. Snickle used her nicest teacher handwriting to write "Fiction" on the label. Then she stuck it on the lower part of the book's spine.

"This way," Ms. Snickle explained, "if anyone ever does read the book, they'll think it's a made-up story, like a fairy tale."

"But don't we need a title?" Lacey asked. "All books have titles."

"That's easy," said Ms. Snickle. She wrote the title carefully and held up the book for everyone to see. It said *The Secrets of Ms. Snickle's Class.*

"ACHOO!" sneezed Hayley.